Cop and Coin
A Novel

R. Scott Lunsford

Cover Design: SelfPubBookCovers.com/INeedABookCover

Editing, review and creative assistance Taryn Aldrich

R. Scott Lunsford

DEDICATION

For the First Responders and all who works to help young and old have a better place in the world.

CONTENTS

R. Scott Lunsford

ACKNOWLEDGMENTS

Thanks to everyone who supported and helped. Robin my patient wife. Alfred, friend, reader, critic, and corrector. Taryn, editresse, and creative consultant/fixer. All the Cops I have known and learned from over the years. A small part of each can be found in Bishop and his peers.

Of course the larger than life real Joshua P. Warren. Researcher, talk show host, author and other skills to numerable to name. Thank you for allowing me to borrow your persona for a while.
www.speakingofstrange.com
www.JoshuaPWarren.com

If the story interests you and makes you curious about the real events, I invite you to investigate for yourself**, "Truth is always strange, stranger than fiction"**. **Lord Byron**

CHAPTER ONE

The Buncombe Turnpike Asheville, NC: 1834

Men are probably nearer the central truth in their superstitions than in their science.

Henry David Thoreau

Thomas Jenkins was trying hard to keep up with his father, but the 12-year-old boy's legs were just not as long. The two were returning home along the dirt Drovers' road, known as the Buncombe Turnpike. It was September, and Thomas' father had sold his share of the large herd of pigs he and neighbors had herded down to Asheville. Drovers herded hogs, turkeys, and produce from as far away as Johnson City, Tennessee to sell at city markets. By selling his stock early to Mr. Smith at the Drovers' stop near the Smith toll bridge over Asheville's French Broad River, Thomas' father had been able to start back home to tend to more pressing matters at his small farm.

They had left the Smith toll bridge late with the intention of spending the night between drover stops. Much like modern truck stops, drover stands were set up about a day's walk apart along the trail. In offering food, lodging, and other supplies for drovers and their stock, the turnpike was its own industry. As the sun dipped behind the mountains, Thomas' father began searching for a side path that seemed familiar. He hoped it would lead to a small campsite he had visited many times before.

Thomas was so absorbed with matching his father's stride amidst the thicket that when he stopped, Thomas stepped right into him. That was when Thomas first noticed the music—music that seemed to roll straight out of the trees. It was a fiddle, lazily playing a tune he had not heard before. It somehow sounded sad, yet strangely ominous at the same time. Peering through the woods, Thomas noticed the titian cast of a fire burning towards the end of the path where he and his father stood. He knew his father was trying to determine if they should travel that way or continue down the turnpike.

"Hello, the fire!" Thomas' father yelled out. Thomas now knew what the decision was. Having traveled the mountains and hills of North Carolina and Tennessee with his family since he was 10 years old, he had learned quickly not to approach someone else's camp without making his presence known first.

The fiddle paused briefly and a baritone voice returned, "Come to the fire." Suddenly the music changed to a more jovial tune as they made their way through the branches. Sitting before the fire with his back to a tree, a haversack and bedroll to his right, was a sight Thomas would remember for the rest of his days. The fiddle player appeared tall and thin. His hair was dark, matched by a days-old beard. He wore a stained brown leather coat that had likely been patched and mended more times than Thomas could count. His boots were obviously newer and did not seem to go with the rest of him.

"Welcome," the man said.

His voice was deep and clear, and when he smiled, Thomas found that the lines around his green eyes lit his whole face. He reminded Thomas of a circuit rider preacher who had passed by the farm once while preaching his way around the mountains. The stranger had two pots hanging near the fire, one with coffee, the other full of what smelled like a weak soup.

He stopped playing his fiddle and stood to offer a gnarled hand to Thomas's father. "James Leeds," he said.

Thomas's father returned the gesture. "Will Gentry. This here's my boy Tom."

The man gave a slight bow and a grin to Thomas.

Thomas smiled back and replied bashfully, "Evening, sir."

"Don't have much to offer you—mostly coffee—but you're welcome to it. The stew's on the lean side. Didn't have much to put in it," Leeds said.

"Much obliged." Thomas' father reached into his own pack and produced a battered tin cup which he dipped into the open pot of coffee, filling it about halfway.

Thomas hung back and scanned the campsite while the two men talked. His father, uncles, and he had stayed in this same camp some time before during return trips along the turnpike. They preferred it to staying at one of the drover stations; not only did they save money, but his family liked to keep to themselves. Thus, Thomas had been a bit surprised when his father followed the trail and its music. But Thomas also knew better than to question him.

Apparently some agreement had been struck between the men. Thomas' father turned to him and said with a pointed finger, "Tom, clean two of those taters and add them to the soup with some onion."

"Yes, sir," Thomas replied.

Thomas hurried to cut the potatoes into neat chunks so they would cook more quickly. He cut and tossed in half an onion then stirred the stew with a forked stick Leeds had in the bigger of the two pots, all the while sneaking side glances at Leeds and the fiddle that never met the ground.

After a meal of soup, hard bread, and coffee, the two men and the young boy sat around the fire in the middle of the clearing. There was a nip in the air that compelled Thomas to hug his jacket tight around his chest. The host picked up his instrument and began to thread a tune that made the well-worn violin wires sing and squeak. Thomas giggled at the face Leeds would pull when he intentionally made a mistake while playing, each time giving Thomas a quick wink with those green eyes that seemed to glow in the firelight.

Finally, being more comfortable, Thomas asked a question. "Mr. Leeds, did your Pa teach you to play the fiddle?"

"Mind your business, boy," his father scolded.

"That's all right," Leeds answered. "It's a bit of a long story if you really want to hear it."

Being chastised once was enough for Thomas, so he looked to his father before answering.

Thomas' father had known men like Leeds before: the type who would do whatever they could to get out of honest work. Many took to making music or spinning tales to amuse others in hopes of picking up a penny or two, or even a sleep in the barn to escape the rain. Some had been rightly talented in their art. In fact, he had seen a few hold a crowd's attention better than most preachers. If Leeds could tell a story as well as he could fiddle, the boy was in for a treat. Thomas' father gave a quick nod to his son, settled against a tree, and went to light his pipe.

Thomas turned back to Leeds and gave an energetic "Yes, sir" with wide eyes.

"No, my Pappy never taught me a thing," Leeds started out. "Ya might say it was more like a distant kin who taught me to fiddle.

"I used to live up north quite a way. My Paw didn't have time to teach much of nothin'. I was just one of 12 youngins they had about the place. It was hard work to keep all 12 of us fed with not much of anything left for anybody. I got tired of

4

never enough and working before the sun got up to way after it went down. So I struck out on my own," Leeds said.

"After many a day of not finding work or even a soul to offer a dry place to lay my head, I found myself in the piney woods alone. Woods like this—" Leeds waved his hand "—only under a dark sky. I kept my fire a-goin' as best I could until I fell asleep. But like fires do, it finally burned down to coal and gave barely any heat and no light at all. Suddenly I was woke by what sounded like a turkey flying down from his roost. I went to poke the fire when I seen I wasn't alone after all. Sat down across my fire pit was a fellow dressed in dark clothes, and I could hardly tell when he stopped being he and started being the pine. The only bright part of him was the red eyes like the stone in the pit. We sat there across from each other for a while and finally he said just one word."

Leeds' voice became deeper and raspy. 'Brother,' the dark man said. He says this, not like he's asking me something, but like a greeting, like 'Howdy, brother.'"

Leeds continued, "I first thought it was one of my brothers from home who'd followed me to try to bring me back or run away from Pa, too. Then I saw it wasn't no brother from home; he was too big for that. So I said, 'Mister, we kin?' You know what he said then?"

Thomas sat upright with his eyes like saucers, hanging on every word as he stammered out a "No, sir."

"He told me we're half-brothers. Different paws but the same ma."

Thomas's father shifted slightly as he puffed on his pipe, seemingly uncomfortable with this apparent infidelity. He cleared his throat and caught Leads' eye in a silent warning.

Leeds smiled and went on. "Well, my half-brother sat there and listened to me tell my tale of having to get away from the family. How no one would hire me or offer help, and how awfully hard work on a farm was. I told him I wished I could do a different job that wasn't so bad."

He let out a throaty laugh. "The dark man with the red eyes, he told me that his paw could help me with a job. I said that would be right nice if he didn't mind. And after talking all night, I ended up falling asleep by the fire," Leeds said.

Leeds recounted how he'd found some food the next morning sitting beside a small pile of firewood left by the dark man. After a quick breakfast, he packed what little he had and headed south, following the dark man's directions. After a days-long trek, he came upon a clearing in the Carolina woods.

"Twas a spot bigger'n where we be now," Leeds noted. "I'd followed the path I was told about 'til I could hear the sounds of a man talking, like he was a general giving orders to his troops."

A sudden gust of wind swept up dirt and twigs, sending them dancing aloft in a breath of smoke from the fire. Thomas following its flight with his eyes, shivering slightly. "It seemed to be speaking a language I'd never heard before. But when I got closer I could only see one man. He walked the edge of a big circle, kicking the ground every couple steps and cursing about somethin."

Thomas sucked in a breath and his eyes grew larger still. "I heard stories 'bout that place," he whispered cautiously. "That's the Devil's tramping ground. You done went and found the tramping ground when the Devil was-a in it?"

As he had been telling the story, Leeds had slowly come to lean closer to Thomas. His voice dropped in timbre as the story went on. At this point, he stretched against the stump he had been resting on and looked at Thomas and asked, "What you know about the Devil's tramping ground?"

Eagerly, Thomas gushed, "Towards the middle of North Carolina there's a circle where nothing grows, no grass, no trees, no nothin'. 'Cause on certain nights the Devil himself comes out and plots his chores and give orders to his demons for the next day. Sir, what'd he look like?"

"Who looked like?" asked Leeds.

"The Devil, sir. What did he look like?"

"What-for you want to know what the Devil looked like, boy?" Leeds sneered.

"Well, if'n I ever meet him, I surely want to know it's him I'm talking to," Thomas responded.

Leeds laughed. "Boy, why, don't you know the Devil don't look like no one man? Nor no one thing. The Devil can be anything he wants to be, anything a man would like to see and any evil that would mess a man up. That's what the Devil looks like."

A hushed "Amen" came from Thomas' father, still slumped against a tree, leisurely smoking his pipe.

"Well, sir, what did he look like that night?" Thomas asked again.

"Say, boy, I'm trying to tell you, but you keep interrupting," replied Leeds, obviously enjoying the attention Thomas was giving him.

"Yes, sir. Sorry, sir."

"He was taller than me, way over six feet. He looked to be about 35 years old, light-colored hair, eyes that glowed green in the moonlight. He had a shiny leather coat, and he was carryin' a twisted oak walking stick. Even in the dark I could see his skin was tanned like he'd been working in the fields under the hot sun. He had a neat beard and mustache. When he smiled, his eyes looked as old as any grandfather I'd ever seen. He saw me and asked why I was there in a loud voice that shook the trees.

"I told him the strange dark man with the red eyes had sent me. That I'd been told he could help me get a job or learn a new trade," Leeds explained. "The tall man put his finger to his chin and walked a time or two around the circle. Suddenly he stopped and stepped to the center of the circle where there was a bag made out of deer hide that I hadn't noticed. He went into the sack and pulled out a fiddle and a bow and handed them to me."

A light breeze trickled again through the trees and sent parched grass scuttling across the bare earth. "'I don't know nothin' about playin' no fiddle,' I told him," Leeds said. "Then the man smiled and reached deeper into the sack and took out a small leather pouch. And he shook out two small silver coins."

Leeds looked straight at Thomas. "Boy, you know your Bible?"

"Yes, sir," replied Thomas.

"You know about Judas, don't you?" Leeds countered.

"Yes, sir," said Thomas again.

"Well, what did they give Judas for betraying Jesus? Do you know?"

"Yes, sir. Thirty pieces of silver."

"Do you remember what happened to Judas and his 30 pieces of silver?" Leeds prodded.

"Yes, sir, he bought a field and hung hisself."

"What do you think happened to those silver coins?"

"Is that what the tall man gave you, sir?" Thomas asked.

"Well, that's what the tall man said. He handed me one of those coins and told me to drop it inside the fiddle," confirmed Leeds. "I did what he told me. I realized I'd known how to fiddle all along, and so I did."

"Lordy, for sure?" Thomas asked, incredulous.

"Well, you heard me play, didn't you?"

"Well, yes, sir," Thomas said.

At that point, Leeds picked up his fiddle and rocked it gently back and forth so Thomas could hear something rattling inside the fiddle box itself.

Was it one of Judas's coins? Thomas wondered. "Golly," he whispered.

Thomas looked to his father who was attempting to relight his pipe on the opposite side of the fire. He looked to be enjoying the story as much as he did the wonder on his son's face.

8

"Mr. Leeds, what did the second coin do?" Thomas asked.

"Well, the tall man said if I kept that second coin and worked for him, I'd never grow old," Leeds replied.

"Oh, Lordy, Mr. Leeds, what type of work did you do for him?"

"Well, all kinds of things: deliver messages, collect on loans, fix problems," Leeds told him. "Why, I do recall once a year or two ago, I happened to help a girl with her baby get rid of a big problem."

"How'd you do that?"

"I burnt part of the problem up in the fireplace, put part of it under the floor, and hid the rest out about in the woods," Leeds said.

At this point, something in the story rang familiar to Thomas' father. He started at the realization and looked straight at Leeds.

"You sayin' you killed Charlie Silver in Morganton? The murder they hung his wife Frankie for?"

"Well, she was no help with it. She just sat on the bed, staring at a spot on the wall. Like she was sleeping sitting up," said a grinning Leeds.

Thomas felt a change of tone in the air around him, but didn't quite understand what was happening. He recalled a song he'd heard before about a woman named Frankie killing her husband, Charlie. As if Leeds were reading his mind, he put the bow to the fiddle and sang two fast verses:

> *This dreadful dark and dismal day*
> *has swept my glories all away.*
> *My sun goes down, my days are past,*
> *and I must leave this world at last!*
> *Oh! Lord, what will become of me?*
> *I am condemned, you all now see,*

to Heaven or Hell my soul must fly
All in a moment when I die...

Setting his fiddle down on the bedroll in front of him, Leeds continued, "Ya see, to keep death away the tall man told me I needed to carry the second coin with me and send him replacements."

Leeds reached down to his belt with his left hand and grasped a greasy, dulled leather pouch. "Every time I kill someone for him, I feel younger and stronger. This way I can best Death himself," Leeds said.

He flipped the bedroll back quickly over the fiddle, revealing two single shot pistols and a knife. Both pistols were already cocked and Leeds grabbed one, pointing it at Thomas' father. "When they hanged Frankie, she got dead and I got more life," Leeds hissed with a sneer.

Thomas was confused by this sudden change of events and sat frozen in front of Leeds, gazing at the pistol aimed at his father. Then his world exploded in movement and sound.

His father hollered, "Run, boy!" and at the same instant got his legs under him and sprang at Leeds like a cat leaping on a barn rat.

Having grown up where his father's orders were followed without question, Thomas jumped up and sprinted for the woods. Out of the corner of his eye, he could see his father freeze in mid-flight as Leeds discharged the pistol into his father's chest. The sound of the weapon's hammer falling with a *click*, followed by a resounding explosion of noise and smoke. The thud of the lead ball hitting his father's abdomen, would forever haunt him.

Leeds dropped that pistol and snatched up the second, turning as the boy ran past him, sighting down the barrel at the boy's back and pulling the trigger. *Click-pop!* The hammer fell but failed to ignite the main charge. Leeds swore loudly and hurled the gun at the running boy.

Thomas had heard many a misfire on handguns and rifles before. He ran faster, knowing it would take a bit of time to reload. The fear of death took over his body as he pumped his legs in his flight away from it.

Thomas had no idea how far he had run or in what direction, dodging trees more by instinct than by sight. He had grown up in the woods, played and hunted there. He thought he would be safe as long as he could stay in them. That's when the ground suddenly vanished from under his feet and he fell. Thomas hit the ground with a thud and found himself in a dry gully. The realization of what had just happened struck him hard. His legs seared with pain, his side throbbed, and scratches ached on his hands and face from ducking through the trees.

Thomas could still hear Leeds far off, cursing everything he saw. "Boy, come back here!" he yelled. "I ain't gonna hurt ya."

But Thomas knew better. The sight of his father dropping like a downed deer, with the sense of finality that death brings, raced through his mind. He knew he had to hide. Thomas began to rake the leaves that filled the gully over himself, starting with his feet and moving up his body. He had done this very thing many times while playing with his cousins back home and had managed to disappear completely.

He could hear Leeds coming and shouting, "Boy, where are you?"

Before camouflaging himself entirely, Thomas peered over the edge of the gully and saw the light of a pine torch through the trees. He tried to be as quiet as he could, measuring his breathing as he listened for Leeds. Before long he heard the footfalls of someone traipsing through the brush. Leeds had stopped yelling for him. Thomas thought he must be trying to track him through the forest, like a hunter would a wounded animal. Then he wondered if he also heard someone else walking on the other side of the gully, but there was no way to be sure.

Oh, Lord, Lord, Thomas thought to himself. *He's got the Devil hisself with him, looking for me. Lord, he's going to find me and kill me, sure enough.*

Thomas felt the fear rising in his chest, tightening its grip. His breath grew fast and shallow. *He might have that other dark man with him, too. The one with the red eyes who called the Devil his paw.* Thomas could hear Leeds's cursed fiddle playing that strange music he had first heard when approaching camp.

If-n I don't stay quiet, they'll find me for sure. Thomas imagined what Leeds and the Devil would do—what had happened to his father, images of the scornful things that might yet befall him. His breath became so rapid that he fainted out of hyperventilation.

CHAPTER TWO
Beside the Buncombe Turnpike: The next morning

Thomas came to as something thudded above him. He could see daylight through the leaves covering his face, but he was afraid to move as the previous night came rushing back to him. He realized the sound of someone, or something, walking around the gully had jarred him from his sleep. Thomas held his breath, hoping either the Devil or Leeds would go away.

And the noise stopped. It sounded like whatever it was loomed right over him. Then he heard the snorting chuckle of the Devil as he realized where Thomas lay under the leaves.

Without warning, the Devil descended upon Thomas in his hiding place in the gully. All Thomas saw was the Devil's massive body and his cloven hooves churning the leaves. He could smell the stench of Hell itself as the Devil shrieked at him, and he knew at that moment there was little left to do than to wait for the end.

***

Samuel Clay had been attempting to catch up with the wandering swine for the past five minutes when it stopped at the edge of a ditch, looked back at Samuel, grunted its disgust with being followed, and lumbered down to investigate. Samuel had heard pigs make all kinds of noises, but the one that arose from the ditch was like nothing he had ever heard before. He wondered if the hog had broken its leg.

Mr. Macintosh was not going to like this. He would take the cost of the hog out of Samuel's pay. Samuel hurried to the side of the ditch and stopped short. The hog appeared to be fine; it lay next to a boy about Samuel's age covered in leaves, seemingly intent on burrowing beside him as if it were a hound trying to get comfortable on its owner's lap.

"Mr. Macintosh! Mr. Macintosh!" Samuel called.

"Boy, just get that hog back to the road. I ain't got no time for your lollygagging," came the reply from the roadway.

"But Mr. Macintosh, your hog done gone and found a dead boy in a ditch!" Samuel yelled.

Hearing this unexpected response to his order, Macintosh and another drover ran to stand with Samuel and stare down at Thomas laying in the ditch, next to a content hog who was apparently planning to spend the rest of the day curled up in the leaves next to the boy.

***

City of Asheville, Buncombe County Courtroom: 1835

Buncombe County Sheriff Willy Jones had had the sort of day he wished never to have again: three hangings all in one shot. He could not recall ever having seen so many people gathered in the same place before. The May sun was hot, and the masses of people had not made it any cooler. If not for Col. Enoch Cunningham, head of the militia guard, it would have surely turned into a lynching rather than a proper hanging. The first two condemned men, Sneed and Henry, had been driven to Gallows Field at East and Sewney Streets chained in the back of a wagon. They had died with a shred of dignity, still claiming to be innocent of their convictions of highway robbery. But the court had found them guilty and their penalty, per the law, was hanging.

Governor Swain was little help, either. In town on state business, he had slipped out yesterday before meeting with the pardon committee that planned to seek clemency for the two men. Sheriff Jones personally thought hanging seemed an excessive punishment for theft, but the law is the law until the government says otherwise.

At the gallows, the preaching went on for quite some time before the trap doors swung open. But it was necessary to teach the crowd about following the rules of man and God—and the consequences that may ensue should they fail to do so.

Jones wished he could have had all three men hanged at once, but his gallows only had two swinging doors. Who would have thought a town like Asheville, in the God-fearing county of Buncombe, would ever need to hang more than two men at the same time? And it was the hanging of the third man that bothered Sheriff Jones the most. For what it was worth, it had been some time coming. Leeds was indeed a strange type. He never spoke a word in his own defense. The lawyer appointed to represent him had even managed to delay the hanging a bit.

The whole time he was in jail, Leeds acted like nothing mattered—as if sooner or later, someone was going to open the door to his cell and let him out. Leeds didn't let off even the slightest trace of fear right up until he was put in the wagon and rolled to Gallows Field. Then reality struck him. He howled with wails and screams, and his flailing against the chains forced Jones' men to carry him up the steps to the gallows. He seemed to be searching the crowd through the ruckus, perhaps looking for some friend or acquaintance. But no accomplice to an escape would have made it past Cunningham and his militiamen.

At one point the sheriff thought Leeds had found the face he sought. As the noose looped around his neck, he focused on a particular spot in the crowd. His smile conveyed some relief, but whatever he saw did not afford him comfort for long. He was calm for merely a moment before roaring even more fiercely than before.

The sheriff read the charges and verdict over Leeds' belligerence. "You promised me!" was the only intelligible thing to come out of Leeds' mouth. Then the trap door opened and the sudden hush of the crowd amplified the *thunk* of dead weight as he tumbled through the door to the end of the rope. The eerie quiet sent a shiver down Jones' back. Leeds flopped and kicked longer than he was used to. Then the body was lowered into the wagon alongside the expired Sneed and Henry. All three were to be carted out behind the brick building that passed for a courthouse to the east of the town square, then on to the potter's field for burial on the other side of the river.

Yet even with their deaths, the sheriff's work with these men remained undone. The personal belongings of each were to be sold to pay for their jail stays and any other expenses incurred while in the town's custody.

Sneed's and Henry's possessions were fairly straightforward: pocket knives, a watch, some tobacco, and their boots. Leeds' property was a different matter entirely. It included a fiddle, two rusty but still usable pistols, a collection of knives, one bedroll, a skillet, two pots, several gold rings and watch chains, and a shoddy leather pouch containing an old coin. The posse that caught Leeds had also found money he had stolen from his victim, the Jenkins man. That, along with Jenkins' pocket knife and a few other items, had already been returned to the man's family.

Oddly, the sheriff had not seen any of the Jenkins kin at the hanging. He had assumed at least some of the family would have attended to see justice done. Thomas, the young boy who had witnessed the killing and hid from Leeds before being discovered by drovers the next morning had testified about the murder and the stories Leeds had told. In truth, their retelling had been the high point of the trial. The boy had told the jury straight-faced that he believed Leeds was working for the Devil. "Supposing he was, it would explain a few things," Sheriff Jones chuckled to himself.

Some of the items found with Leeds at his main camp had been identified as belonging to others who had either turned up missing over the years or moved on, never to be heard from again. Sheriff Jones figured at least 14 or 15 lost souls were Leeds' possible victims, the "Devil man" as the Jenkins boy had called him on the stand.

The boy's testimony had created quite a stir in the courtroom, as his father's killing and robbery remained the only murder with which the state could officially charge Leeds. Jones was certain Leeds had killed others, but he had no proof.

However, the idea that Leeds had had a hand in Frankie Silvers killing her husband in Morganton, NC was absurd. The court had found her guilty and punished her by hanging just like Leeds, and that was that. There had been talk of Frankie's family coming from Morganton to watch the hanging, but the sheriff hadn't met any of them. Meanwhile, the eastern newspapers had run away with the trial and hanging that was to take place. Word had gotten around the state, not to mention South Carolina and Tennessee, which brought the curious to Asheville in droves.

Printed interviews and stories about Leeds speculated he must have been the half-brother of something called the Jersey Devil, and that he had to be at least 80 judging from so-called relatives interviewed up north. But by looking at him you could tell he was in his mid-20s, not elderly.

Sheriff Jones wasn't known for being superstitious. He was a christian man, but the whole Leeds business admittedly made him a tad nervous. *It was all nonsense—just stories*, he reassured himself. After all, the newspapers were no better than Leeds was, a good-for-nothing storyteller who sang for his supper to avoid having to make a living. But then again, newspaper stories didn't kill people.

As his thoughts returned to the red brick courthouse, Jones heard boots crossing the rough wooden floor of the courtroom and turned to see Col. Cunningham followed by a parade of other men: John Patton, headmaster of the Newton Academy; John Woodfin, chairman of the Buncombe Co. court; Rev. Thomas Stradley and Rev. Joseph Haskew, who had both led the services at the hanging; and finally Joshua Roberts, Leeds' lawyer.

Col. Cunningham opened the conversation. "Willy, can we have a word?"

"Gentlemen, what can I do for you?" the sheriff responded.

"We wanted to speak to you about Leeds."

The sheriff shifted on his feet. He should've known it wasn't over for the day. "Peculiar man, that Leeds. I've seen many men go to their death before, but none how he did."

Reverend Haskew, a tall, lanky man and popular Methodist circuit rider known for his sense of humor, drew back the chair marked for the prosecuting attorney and took a seat. His bowleggedness from circuit riding was clear whenever he sat down. One story often told of the popular Reverend came about from a ride through the countryside on his way to church, where he happened upon two men digging dirt to throw up an embankment to damn a creek. "You men are violating the Sabbath," he had told them. "You'd better quit and come with me to church."

One told him that he and his comrade were preparing a pool for an evening baptism, that it was a case of taking the ass out of the ditch on Sunday. The good Rev. had replied, "It seems to me that instead of taking the ass out of the ditch, you are getting ready to throw him in."

Today, though, Rev. Haskew was not so jovial. "Leeds knew what was waiting for him," he declared. "That was the face of a man who had made a deal with the Devil." The sheriff looked at him. "Reverend, you don't really believe that nonsense the boy said in court. What those papers printed. Do you?"

Reverend Stradley joined his colleague in a nearby seat. "You of all people, Willy, don't believe in the Devil? What have you been doing in that pew every Sunday? Sleeping?"

"'Course there's a Devil," the sheriff conceded, "just not like that boy's story and what they put in the papers."

Col. Cunningham interjected from the corner, his voice ricocheting off the rough floor and brick walls. "You can't tell me you don't believe that some northern devil from New Jersey told Leeds to come to North Carolina to the Devil's tramping ground and get a job working for the Devil himself?" He paused. "Willy, Napoleon's older brother, Joseph Bonaparte, former king of Spain... he thought that the red-eyed demon was real. Said he had spotted the dammed thing when he was huntin' in Bordentown, New Jersey, his huntin party tried to shoot it but missed."

"Willy, Commodore Stephen Decatur, Hero of the 1812 war, visited Hanover Iron Works in New Jersey to test cannonballs," John Patton added. "He, too, said he saw a strange creature flying overhead. Claimed to have put a hole in its wing straight from the cannon, but it kept on going. Didn't seem to be hurt." He huffed. "Bonaparte and Decatur, both good Freemasons. Not lunatics."

The sheriff considered this and looked at John Woodfin, expecting more to the story.

"Willy, where are Leeds's belongings?" came the reply instead.

"Behind the judge's bench in that trunk there," the sheriff answered.

Cunningham hauled the chest over and put it on the defendant's table. The sheriff produced a ring of iron keys and opened the wooden chest to reveal Mr. Leeds's last effects.

Leeds's attorney approached the box and pulled out the fiddle and bow. Roberts laid them on the table along with the worn leather pouch. Out of the pouch came a single coin, which he placed beside the instrument.

19

Patton plucked up the tarnished disk and studied it, stating, "It looks like an old coin."

Rev. Haskew took the coin from him to quote a Bible verse. "Then one of the 12, called Judas Iscariot, went unto the chief priests, and said unto them, 'What will ye give me, and I will deliver him unto you?' And they covenanted with him for 30 pieces of silver, Matthew 26. And the Book of John tells us that Judas carried the disciples' money bag and betrayed Jesus for a bribe of thirty pieces of silver."

Rev. Stradley, a devout Baptist, naturally refused to be outdone by his Methodist friend and pointed out, "That would be a silver shekel you're holding there, John. The Gospel of Matthew says that, after Jesus was arrested by the Romans, Judas gave back the bribe to the Jewish priests and committed suicide by hanging. The priests used the bribe to buy a potter's field. The Acts of the Apostles tells us that Judas used the bribe to buy a field, but fell down headfirst, and burst asunder in the midst."

Jones stood observing all this, more than a little amused. "You all don't really think that coin was part of the bribe paid to Judas, do ya?" Pointing towards the table piled with Leeds' possessions, the sheriff pondered aloud, "How in the world would a shekel talked about in the Bible get all the way here to the mountains in North Carolina?"

Patton glanced at Roberts and asked, "You didn't tell him?"

"Well, no, I thought his deputy had told him before now."

"Told me what, exactly?" Jones questioned.

Roberts sat forward and explained, "When I was preparing for the trial, I met with Leeds to review testimony and evidence. I hope I never meet as arrogant a man again. What he asked for most was his fiddle and that little pouch there, but he knew he wouldn't get them back unless he was acquitted. And he was convinced any conviction would be overturned. Not by the Governor... but he wouldn't tell me who."

The sheriff put a stop to Roberts' story and said, "What about my deputy? Which one you talkin' about?"

"Deputy Clark"

"*George* Clark? What's he got to do with this? He quit before the trial was over and moved back to Virginia. Said he had to take care of an ill relative or something."

"Sometimes when I came to speak with Leeds, I'd catch Deputy Clark taunting him with the fiddle. One day there was a weird tune playing when I got to the jail. I thought Clark had finally let Leeds have his fiddle back, but it turned out that Clark was playing the fiddle in front of Leeds's cell while he sat there with a huge grin on his face. I asked him what song he was playing, but he couldn't name it. And then the deputy wouldn't talk about the damn fiddle anymore."

Genuinely puzzled, Jones stated, "But I've known Clark since he was a boy. He couldn't carry a tune in a bucket, much less play a fiddle."

Col. Cunningham took the fiddle from the table and rocked it, sliding whatever rested in its sound box to and fro.

"Oh, really, now," the sheriff sighed, exasperated. "You two don't think this Devil nonsense is true?"

"Clark told me about playing the fiddle before he left for Virginia, Sheriff," John Patton said earnestly. "And I listened. He went to Newton; wasn't known for tall tales. I guess Leeds talked to him when he was on night duty, telling him the same stories he told the Jenkins boy about traveling and doing the Devil's work. The deputy was convinced Leeds believed the stories. Even that the Devil himself would be coming soon to free him so he could get back to work. It was one of the reasons he wanted his coins back. But Clark thought Leeds was just insane... at least until he got hold of the fiddle and found he could play it. That's why Clark left town after we talked. Said he had to get as far away from Leeds, his green eyes and fiddle as he could."

Pointing at Col. Cunningham and Headmaster Patton, the sheriff countered, "You both were with me when we brought Leeds in after they found the Jenkins boy and his daddy's body. Did you see anything that made you think he was more than a madman, a killer, a thief?"

Col. Cunningham, who had proven instrumental in preventing a lynching right that very night so they could bring back Leeds alive for trial, spoke up then. "We thought he was a murderer and thief, plain and simple, but you yourself, Sheriff, told me you thought he'd killed more than just the Jenkins man. The beating he got from some of our men before we pulled them off should have killed him outright anyway. Order out of chaos takes some time to establish."

"But the other belongings here had to be the property of someone," Jones said, waving at the items still in the trunk on the table.

"I made some inquiries of my own through various sources, including Governor Swain, who also questioned whoever he had access to. Your guest, Sheriff, may have indeed been close to 100 years old." Col. Cunningham added, "Leeds's name was found in court records in New Bern from 30 years ago. And as far as this half-brother issue is concerned, as I understand it, a woman called Mother Leeds had 12 children and said if she had another, it would be the Devil. She was assumed to be Deborah Leeds, the wife of Japhet Leeds. In 1736, he drafted a will that's still listed by the court clerk in New Jersey. It names twelve children, and the youngest is James Leeds. Number 13 is figured to be the creature our good brothers-in-arms saw."

"Right. Nice bedtime stories," the sheriff quipped, "but what does all this have to do with us? Leeds is dead and if what you say is true, he's having whiskey with his boss in Hell right now."

John Woodfin piped up with, "It's about the coins. They have to be kept safe where they won't cause any harm. That's why the Governor was here, and why he left before the hanging. He had to separate the state from this business, true or not, for the safety of the people."

Sheriff Jones had had quite enough of this drivel and was going to put an end to it and said so. He grabbed the fiddle from Col. Cunningham with one hand and retrieved the bow with the other. "So by your reckoning," he said, "I should be able to play this thing while the coin is in it." He put the instrument to his left shoulder, raised the bow with his right hand, and went to place the bow to string. Suddenly he froze, captivated by the fingers on his left hand that had poised themselves above the threads. He had never picked up a fiddle in his life, yet here he was holding one in what seemed to be a natural way. The sheriff somehow knew that if he let the bow down, he would play even though he never had before. He knew not why or how, but he was certain he could. He lowered the bow and placed both it and the fiddle back on the table. The other gentlemen in the room realized they had been holding their breath and released a collective sigh.

The sheriff peered at the instrument on the table and simply said, "Brothers, what do we have to do?"

All eyes turned to John Patton, who suggested, "Gentlemen, we need to seek out the bravest of the brave."

CHAPTER THREE
Luxembourg Palace Gardens, France: December 7, 1815

The tranquility of the pristine garden dissipated with the rhythmic stomps of soldiers forming a line for the firing squad. General Victor Rochechouart watched while his aide, Col. Auguste LaRochejacquelein, stood observing the men before him in the rain.

A tall man with red hair entered the space, seeming to ignore the weather as he marched instead with an air of defiance. Taking note of the General, the man presented himself with a salute. The two spoke briefly before the General nodded and the man counted off 12 paces that brought him face-to-face with the double line of soldiers.

This man, the one who Napoleon himself had called the "bravest of the brave", had been convicted of high treason against the French state and its Bourbon king, Louis XVIII. The sergeant barked out an order that brought every soldier to attention. All was silent save for the drips of rain from officers' caps and visors.

Major de Saint Bias delivered the command: "Ready… aim…" The firing squad's rifles were trained on Field Marshal Michel Ney who himself gave the finial command. "…Fire!" The Marshall brought his hand swiftly to his chest.

Muskets clicked, then erupted as acrid smoke veiled the damp greenery of the garden. Field Marshall Michel Ney fell immediately, fresh crimson leaking onto the flagstones.

A cry rose from the small crowd of civilians in the garden. "They've killed Marshal Ney!"

The body was carried off the grounds to a hospital nearby, followed by submission of a report to King Louis. All twelve rounds had found their mark, it said, and the King accepted swiftly the news of Ney's execution.

Per the King's orders, the marshal's body was sent in secret to Père Lachaise cemetery in Paris. His wife did not attend the burial. A representative of the English Duke of Wellington would later call upon Madame Ney at her Paris apartment the evening of the funeral. "Madame Ney, the Duke of Wellington sends his condolences in your time of loss."

"Please advise the Duke that I thank him," she responded. "And please also thank him for all he has done for the Ney family."

"Of course, Madame Ney. There is a long-standing tradition of looking after a brother Mason and his family in times of need." The officer offered a quick salute and turned on his heel, leaving Madame Ney to her own thoughts.

It was still raining early in the morning at a distant French port. As a ship bound for America prepared to leave with the tide, a brooding, auburn-haired man with a dye-splattered shirt climbed aboard and was whisked below deck.

***

Charleston Harbor, SC: January 1816

Tall redheaded French fencing master and teacher Peter Stuart Ney had just disembarked from a ship from France. He was welcomed in the briny air by members of the local Masonic Lodge who brought him back to their homes in Charleston one by one. Some claim that thanks to the assistance of St. John's Masonic Lodge members, countless numbers of Napoleon's French military officers have entered the U.S. via various ports including Baltimore, Philadelphia, and Charleston. Many choose to disappear into the countryside, mostly to join established French communities in South Carolina and Louisiana.

Napoleon's Marshal Michel Ney was reported to have last been seen by French refugees in Georgetown in 1819, and Mr. Peter Ney was said to have left the Georgetown area around this same time. Napoleon's Marshal was not spied in the coastal community again. Mr. Peter Ney apparently took a teaching job in Brownsville, SC in 1820. From there, he moved to Mocksville, NC, and then to Third Creek, NC to teach the young men of the community.

In 1835, a 67-year-old Peter Ney decided to pay a visit to Asheville. A coach on the stage line of Messers, Baxter, & Adams pulled up in front of the Sulphur Springs Hotel, from which several guests emerged anticipating a stay at Asheville's first-ever health resort. The modest white clapboard building stood about five miles west of the city square.

Mr. Ney was the last to climb out of the coach. Straightening up on the front stoop of the hotel, he cursed the inventor of the bouncing box on wheels in which he had been forced to ride from Morganton. "Man was meant to ride upon a horse, not to be dragged across the mountains behind them," he muttered as he rubbed life back into his stiff limbs.

A large black man came from the side of the main building and proceeded to manhandle passengers' bags to wrangle them into the hotel.

Ney hollered out, "You there! Take care; I have good brandy in that bag."

"Yes, sir," came the dutiful response.

"You do, and I'll be inclined to share a glass in the evening with a man who takes pride in his work." The bellboy's face lit up at Ney's suggestion. He smiled back before loping up the steps to the covered porch to check into the hotel.

Two days later, a horse and buggy helmed by two men and a single rider approached the hotel. Col. Reuben Deaver, the establishment's owner and builder, met the men on the porch. Col. Cunningham dismounted his horse as John Patton and John Woodfin lowered themselves one at a time from the buggy.

The newcomers exchanged pleasantries with Col. Deaver before Col. Cunningham inquired, "Did Mr. Ney arrive?"

"Yes, he's here, and I haven't been able to get any work out of my musicians since," Col. Deaver replied. The Sulfur Springs Hotel boasted an expansive ballroom outfitted with a crystal chandelier and polished wooden floor. A string band composed of free Negroes from Charleston and Columbia provided the music for dancing in the evening.

"One of my players, Lapitude, and Mr. Ney have been involved in a game of chess or an argument over Napoleon or some such almost constantly since his arrival. Gentlemen, come inside and see for yourselves."

The four men entered the hotel and were led to the parlor where an older gentleman sat across from a younger black man with a chess board between them. A second black man, seated in the middle, leaned back in his chair with a smile on his face and his arms crossed. Both were wearing matching jackets and trousers. The older white man lectured as the game went on, teasing his opponent that he must be deaf as he had just explained a specific point the previous night. A smile crept across his face as he suddenly stopped to survey the chess board and noticed the position of one of the other player's pieces.

"A diversion, Lapitude? No such luck, my friend." Ney made a move with his rook and declared, "Checkmate."

His opponent smirked. "Almost had ya, sir."

The observer in the middle laughed and added, "I do like it when he flusters you, Captain."

Col. Deaver snuck into the conversation. "Lapitude, you and Randall have guests wanting some music this evening. And you know some of the guests don't like seeing you two in the parlor."

Ney stood and turned to the newcomers. "Guests be damned," he said with a sweep of his hand. "This is chess, sir."

"We're a-going. Another game in the morning, Mr. Ney?" Lapitude offered.

He shook his head, sizing up the men who had entered alongside Col. Deaver. "No, I believe I may be leaving in the morning. My invitation, though, still stands."

"Think you, sir." And with that, the two young men walked out towards the hotel's ballroom and their waiting guests.

Ney sat down again and proceeded to put the chess pieces back in their original places on the chess board. "Interesting pair, don't you think?" He nodded in the direction of the absent musicians. "Latitude owns a plantation near Charleston that's worked by forty men, and his friend Randall earned an award of $5,000 last year from the people of South Carolina for his assistance in a riot situation in the city. Very talented musicians as well. Wouldn't you agree, Col. Deaver?"

"That's what I pay them for, Mr. Ney."

Ney indicated chairs for the newcomers, saying, "Sit, gentlemen, we have business to discuss."

Col. Cunningham, Woodfin, and Patton all took chairs around the chess table with Col. Cunningham making introductions. Then Ney was the first to speak. "I have read your letters with interest. You are quite sure of this, gentlemen?"

Patton slipped a small leather pouch from an interior jacket pocket and placed it atop the chess board. Ney picked it up and removed two tarnished disks for examination. Ever the historian, he assumed a teaching stance as he twirled the metal rounds with his fingers, explaining, "The '30 pieces of silver' paid to Judas to betray Christ were shekels from the ancient city of Tyre. They were handmade in Jerusalem. The Shekel of Tyre appears in several Biblical stories; it was the only coin accepted as payment for the annual Jewish temple tax. And it was also the coin found in the mouth of a fish that was to be used by Jesus and His disciples to pay for the temple tax, according to the gospel of Matthew. But most famously, it was used to pay Judas Iscariot his 30 pieces of silver for betraying his Lord. This one—" he held up a coin "—appears to have been worn down more than the other, I would assume from more handling." He scanned the men's faces curiously before continuing. "You realize, of course, the existence of these coins is not so unusual?"

Ney tapped his chin thoughtfully. "I've heard stories in Europe of other coins and relics. And I've seen the Lance of Longinus myself, which is the spear that pierced Christ's side— or at least the point of the lance. The blade of the lance is set in an icon and was brought by the King from Constantinople to be enshrined in the Saints' Chapel in Paris." Ney slid the coins back onto the chess board. "And the instrument you wrote about?"

"Burned," Patton replied.

"I see. Were you able to fulfill my requests?"

Col. Cunningham reached into his jacket pocket and pulled out a small metal box, about two by four inches, which he placed on the board beside the coins.

"I believe you were wise to see that these relics are secured. I understand there has been much death connected to them."

Woodfin nodded, saying, "Our Sheriff estimates 14. Possibly more based on the items Leeds had in his camp and on his person when he was caught."

"Yes, Mr. James Leeds. You have made a connection to the North?"

"We believe so, according to information the Governor has obtained."

"It's an amazing story, no?"

"I am surprised Bonaparte didn't bring down that creature when his hunting party had a chance," Patton scoffed.

"Joseph is an excellent shot," Ney remarked, referring to Joseph Bonaparte, brother of Napoleon. "If he'd had a good field of fire, he would have brought it down, I'm sure. And is there anyone else who is aware of this situation?"

"Just those that need to know. The fewer the better so as not to start rumors."

"Yes, I agree," Ney said, "but then again, I don't quite understand. Why not just take the coins and drop them in the ocean? Would that not have solved the problem and removed their influence from the hands of man?"

"We had discussed that, Mr. Ney," Col. Cunningham assured him. "However, there have been several instances of gold coins from Spanish shipwrecks washing up on the Carolina shore after storms. It was decided that chance could not be taken, but someone who could be trusted to keep the coins safe needed to be found. If there is an evil persona that goes with the coins, we can keep others safe as well."

Ney arched a brow and queried, "So are you familiar with the stories of other Judas coins from long ago?" Given the men's relative ignorance and the time they had, he decided to share a few tales. The first concerned an Irish man named Jack, a thief who allegedly earned his expert thieving prowess from a coin he carried that had been traded with the Devil at a crossroads in Ireland. Some of his riches were to be returned to the Devil to keep him at bay and save Jack's soul from Hell. When Jack eventually died, he failed to gain entrance into Heaven because of his sins. Yet the Devil, true to his word, refused to welcome Jack into Hell either, sending him instead back into the night to wander purgatory for eternity. When Jack complained it was too dark to see, the Devil gave him a burning ember and as it was from hell it was an eternal flame. It has been said that the light from Hell's ember can often be seen throughout the countryside of Ireland. "And interestingly," Ney said, "it seems many stories like this have some small grain of truth to them."

Another instance, with which Ney was personally familiar, involved the cathedral of Aachen in Germany. "I am aware Napoleon's troops took a beautiful statue of a wolf from the cathedral of Aachen to Paris. "I spoke to a priest there myself who related the story of how the magnificent cathedral was built," he began. The townsfolk had long hoped to build a massive church, and its construction plans soon consumed the city. Over time, though, money for the holy work ran out. Craftsmen moved on to other projects once the cathedral plans were suspended. And so the church's skeleton stood incomplete, more reminiscent of ancient ruins than a glorious cathedral. Town leaders were flummoxed. They endeavored to borrow funds, but rich patrons were reluctant to donate to the cause. Community collections also produced little; residents were largely poor. Even churchgoers, who would generally be the first to contribute to funding a house of God, gave paltry sums. When the town mayor received this report, he and his council were dumbfounded and could do little more than gaze despondently at the unfinished cathedral walls, just as fathers would look upon sick children they could not heal.

"But one day," Ney explained, "a mysterious stranger arrived in town." The man was said to be striking, with dark skin and bright flashing green eyes, and offered the councilmen silver and gold coins to support further construction of their much-wished-for edifice. The mayor was especially suspicious of this sudden hero, and understandably so. 'My Noble Lord, who are you'," Ney recounted the man as saying, "'who speaks of coins as though they were sacks of beans? Pray tell us your name, your rank in this world, and whether you are sent from on high to assist.'"

Ney continued, "The man was evasive. He told the councilmen, 'I do not reside there and have not for a very long time, and I ask that you don't trouble yourselves with questions concerning who and what I am. Only know that I have coin as plentiful as the stars in the summer sky.' As he withdrew a small pouch containing 20 silver coins that had purchased a potter's field in the Far East in decades past, he proposed a deal: 'All these can and shall remain yours if you promise me the first little soul to be consecrated in your new temple.'"

"But who was this stranger, Ney?" Patton asked.

"None else but the Devil himself," Ney replied. "And he advised those men, as they shook at the realization of his identity, not to be afraid. After all, it would be the Devil who would suffer with this contract, not them. He was asking for a single soul in exchange for a bounty of coins. And history has shown that a good King will order a whole army to war to be sacrificed on behalf of his community, yet the councilmen were reluctant to offer only one. And it would likely be that of a hypocrite, because as the Devil explained, we all know he is the first to enter a church."

Patton stroked his chin. "And so what became of the men's conundrum?"

"Well," Ney said, "Scarcely had they agreed to the bargain before the tall man brought forth another, larger sack of coins and took his leave. And the cursed silver and gold was indeed used to finish the cathedral, but when the building was completed, striking though it was, the town was filled with fear at the sight of it. Even though the council had sworn not to divulge the contract, it seems that one of the elders had told his wife, and she had carried the word to the market. The news spread like wildfire, to the point that no one dared step foot in the church."

"...Which means no soul could be sacrificed in exchange," Patton concluded.

"You would be correct, sir," Ney agreed. "But when the council consulted the Church for an answer, an old wise monk had a suggestion. The wolf that had been ravaging people's crops had just been caught alive. Surely the Devil expected the soul of the first entrant to the church, but of whom or what was never specified. So the town elders decided to execute this cunning trick: orders were given to bring the wolf to the cathedral entrance, and just as the bells began to toll, the trap door of the cage swung open and the beast hurtled out into the nave of the empty church. But Satan beheld the offering with a terrible fury. He was enraged that the master of deception himself had been deceived, and he slammed the great brass gates to the church entrance so violently that the gate cracked in two. In fact, his thumb was torn off by the force. And legend has it his thumb can still be felt to this day in one of the two lions' heads that grace the bronze gates.

"I have seen and touched this crack that commemorates the monk's victory over the Devil, as can anyone who wishes to visit the church," Ney declared proudly. "And to be honest, whether these stories are true or not, the connection of these coins with evil and death is a fact."

"So it is necessary to keep the coins in a safe place, away from innocent people," said Woodfin.

"*Oui,* but of course," Ney replied. "Better safe than sorry, yes?"

"Indeed, Mr. Ney, but are you the gentleman for this task? Thieves and highwaymen are known to be about.

With his left hand, Ney retrieved his walking stick that had been leaning against the polished table. He grasped the hilt of the cane and pulled out a blade encased in its wooden shaft. In one fluid move, Ney tuned at the waist, extended his arm and with a flick of his wrist sliced a candle in two, in a holder on a side table. With almost the same speed the blade disappeared back into the cane's shaft. "You do realize with whom you speak, sir?" Ney said with a smile.

Patton promised, "Yes, better than most."

"But Mr. Ney," Col. Cunningham asked, "why the iron box?"

Ney picked up the coins and placed them back into the leather pouch, then opened the small iron box and tucked it inside. "I think it might be best not to handle the items in question, but for my own good." Ney nestled the box into his jacket pocket. "Gentlemen, care to join me in the ballroom to enjoy some music?"

"Well, sir, I believe we will be heading back to Asheville as the matter at hand is finished," Col. Cunningham responded.

"A shame. Excellent music, if I do say so. Worry not; I will see to the safe keeping of the items of concern." Ney stood with authority and headed in the direction of the ballroom accompanied by his host, Col. Deaver. The other three gentlemen departed to meet their transportation back to Asheville.

CHAPTER FOUR
Riverside Cemetery: April 1894

Robert Vance considered it something never to occur again: ten thousand people swarming Asheville's city center in a mile-long procession to Riverside Cemetery. The former governor and current senator Zebulon "Zeb" Baird Vance had died.

His heart had given out April 14, 1894, while he was serving in the U.S. Senate in Washington, D.C. At the insistence of his wife and over the objections of the Vance family, Zeb would not have a Masonic funeral. Zeb's second wife, Florence, had not come from a Masonic family like his first wife Hattie. Even so, 120 Masons had rehearsed the funeral at Asheville's Mount Hermon Lodge in preparation for the proper burial due every Mason.

They trekked as a group in the rain alongside rich and poor, black and white, parents and children. All felt the pain of having lost a personal friend. Although the funeral service was not Masonic, something strange did occur that went largely unnoticed by the attendees. Zeb's brother Bob, who had become N.C. Grand Master of Masons, placed a small iron box on top of the coffin to be buried with the Great Leader of N.C. It was decided that Zeb had been so revered in life that no one would disturb him in death. Fitting, then, that even in the afterlife Zeb would oversee the box and its contents, just as he had for many years.

Bob Vance couldn't help but wonder if it was more than the call of duty that led Zeb to ensure the security of that small box and whatever was held within. The box was but spoken of only once between the brothers, and just long enough for Zeb to explain that the box and its contents had afforded him a personal understanding of evil and an unrelenting resolve to protect others from it.

Bob Vance had been 18 years old when he was called to Third Creek, N. C. upon Mr. Peter Stuart Ney's passing. Before he died, Ney had requested that an envelope atop his desk be given to Bob Vance in Asheville, detailing the location of the room he rented where he kept additional documentation and a small iron box. Mr. Ney had written to Bob's father, Dr. Vance, many times before the doctor died in a duel outside of Saluda, NC. This exchange of goods had therefore been planned far in advance of Ney's death in his collaboration with several important figures in the Asheville community.

Upon arriving at Third Creek, Vance inquired if Ney had left any other instructions for him and was only told that on his deathbed, the 77-year-old Ney was asked by his doctor if he was in fact Napoleon's famous general, the "bravest of the brave." Ney allegedly propped himself up on one elbow and declared, "I will not die with a lie on my lips. By all that is holy, I am Marshal Ney of France" And thus passed Peter Stuart Ney, teacher and mentor of many a young man from Third Creek, and formerly Napoleon's Marshal Ney of France.

Armed with this story, the written directions from the former marshal, and the small iron box, Vance returned to Asheville where his family became the guardians of the box and its contents. This ownership continued without incident until the War Between the States.

For various reasons, Zeb was later given charge over the box. It was during this time that one of the silver coins, either by theft or by accident, became separated from its twin and ended up in the custody of Private Thomas C. Dula of Company K of the 42nd Regiment, N.C. troops. Private Dula made it through some of the worst fighting and skirmishes of the war without a scratch. He attributed his longevity to his good luck charm, a silver coin he carried through the war that he claimed to have found on a battlefield. Dula told anyone who would listen, "Every Yankee I sent to Hell on the battlefield made me feel better, stronger, and luckier."

After the war, Dula returned home to Watauga County, NC to find that his former girl had married someone else under the assumption that Dula, like most men, would never return. Wishing her the best in her future, he gifted her his lucky coin and soon took up with his former girlfriend's younger cousin, Laura Foster. In May 1866, Laura Foster disappeared. Her pregnant body was found after some time in a shallow grave, her death the result of multiple stab wounds to the chest. Dula, who had fled to Tennessee, was extradited to North Carolina to face charges upon learning of the death.

After Dula was arrested, Zeb Vance (the state's governor at the time) represented Dula *pro bono* and maintained the man's innocence. Zeb succeeded in having the trial moved from Wilkesboro to Statesville, NC as it was widely believed that Dula would never receive a fair trial in Wilkes County. Dula was nevertheless convicted not once but twice, first at the initial trial and again following his appeal.

On May 1, 1868, Dula was hanged in Statesville. By that time the case had drawn widespread attention. Many in the community defended Dula, arguing that he took the fall for his first love Ann Melton, who had killed Laura Foster in a fit of rage over having lost Dula to her. This story of love, loss, and tragedy interested nearly everyone who heard it, and those who did always suspected there was more to the story than what was common knowledge. It even became the basis for the popular folk song, "Tom Dooley."

Zeb kept hold of the missing coin after the trial by confronting Melton and returning it to its place beside the other in the iron box, vowing never to allow it to go asunder while he was alive—and he kept his promise. Many believed the same would be true after his death as well. Florence, however, had other ideas. After a widely publicized funeral, she had Zeb secretly exhumed and reburied so he would spend eternity next to her and her family instead of his first wife.

When Zeb's brother caught wind of the purported switch, he directed one of his men to drive a long iron rod into the original grave to confirm the missing casket. Bob then obtained a court order to move him back to his intended plot, and now here they were again laying his brother to rest a third time. Bob chuckled to himself that even in death, his brother was as much a traveling man as he was in life.

The difference this time would be in not placing the small iron box on top of the casket. When Zeb was exhumed, the box was on the casket in the second grave just as it had been originally. Yet when the box was opened, only one coin remained in the leather pouch. The men who had been hired by his second wife to move the former governor after his funeral were interrogated nearly endlessly but denied any knowledge of the coin. They simply claimed to have placed the iron box on the casket undisturbed from its intended place out of respect for the former governor. This thought made Vance smile. Indeed, there was a lot of respect in moving his brother in the first place. Respect for money, perhaps. Part of the justice being done today was in making the same men dig up and return his brother to his original resting place.

After the latest burial, a new, safer location for the remaining coin would need to be determined. The fate of the missing coin was to be investigated as well. Unfortunately, Bob and his nephews were again disappointed that even this third burial would not follow Masonic rites.

After much debate amongst some of the most influential men in Asheville, it was decided that Zeb remained the ideal guardian of the box and its contents, albeit indirectly. A monument to Zeb would be erected of massive stone and the box placed under its great weight where all could look upon the monument and recall a great leader of the state and excellent brother mason. However, those who knew of the box's existence could rest assured that as long as the monument stood, the forces of physics would keep the small iron box safely away from the hands of man.

Two years after Zeb's death in 1894, George W. Pack, a fellow Mason and successful Asheville businessman, donated $2,000 to help pay for the monument. It was designed by Richard Sharp Smith, otherwise known as the wealthy George Vanderbilt's architect who had worked on Vanderbilt's Biltmore House and estate in Asheville. The cornerstone of the monument was set on the winter solstice in 1897 in a public Masonic ritual.

By 1898, the monument was complete with a 10-story obelisk dedicated to Zeb placed in the city square for all to see. Famous for his speech "The Scattered Nation" in which he spoke of "the wickedness and the folly of intolerance", Zeb was honored by the local chapter of the United Daughters of the Confederacy and the local chapter of B'nai B'rith at a yearly ceremony held at the foot of the Vance Monument. Yet even as a statesman known for his work during the Civil War and thereafter to prevent anti-Semitic prejudice, very few realized that the famous gentleman used his presence to keep evil from man's hands and inside a small iron box beneath the monument bearing his name.

***

Asheville: September 1902

As rumor and legends are wont to do, the stories of the coins were further spread by men sworn to secrecy. For as Benjamin Franklin said through Poor Richard in 1735, "Three may keep a secret, if two of them are dead."

The story of the missing Judas coin had traveled far beyond the mountains of Western N.C., with lore of its abilities growing ever steadily over time. The coin was said to provide eternal life or untouchable knowledge to those who held it, luck to those who lived life as a risk, and the ability to cure illness. This latter power combined with the coin's last sighting in the mountains of N.C., already known for its curative air and water, brought many to the land of the sky in search of relief from what ailed them.

Ponce de Leon was said to have traveled these rolling hills in search of his fountain of youth. The valley of Asheville was in fact considered sacred to the local Cherokee Native Americans. Men from all over the world traveled to this region in search of something missing in their own lives; some found it, but others failed. Many left only to find themselves strangely drawn back to these mountains later in life, where they would finish their days as citizens of the valley.

Though he had not started his life here, the stranger who arrived by train in September of 1902 was determined to find the solution to his own imminent demise. Mr. Charles J. Asquith had been recently diagnosed with tuberculosis. Doctors warned he did not have much longer to live before the persistent cough claimed him. The Asheville residents who noted his arrival could see that the English gentleman was not well. He came with doctor and nurse in tow; however, his genteel nature was just as evident as his poor health. With his Vandyke-style raven beard and bowler hat, onlookers thought Asquith may be here to visit or do business with Mr. George Vanderbilt at his fine Biltmore mansion. In the meantime, Asquith took up residence at one of the finer boarding houses on Montford Avenue, north of the sprawling city square, along with his private nurse.

But peculiarly, the distinguished gentleman did not call on the Biltmore or any of the other rich and famous residing in Asheville. Instead, Asquith made inquiries with the working-class in town. His questions were at first unusually broad, as if he were seeking an old friend who had fallen out of touch over the years. His probing then became more pointed: requesting a particular person by name, even offering to pay to meet him at Asquith's boarding room as soon as possible. After an exhausting 10 days' worth of inquisitions, Asquith finally received word that his intended person had been found and was on the way to meet with him. Yet Asquith was increasingly unwell; breathing and moving nearly escaped him. Per his request, the nurse placed him in a chair facing west out of his window so that he could observe the mimosa sundown and contemplate how many more he might live to see.

Asquith's expertise in cheating others out of money and wares did him no good in this fight. In years past, he had managed to talk his way into and out of most anything: court, prison, even marriages to name a few. He loved to gamble, and this trip represented a grand risk that also bore the greatest potential payoff. When pretending to be a reformed man of God while imprisoned in Georgia, locked up for various confidence schemes and frauds, he had told many a man that his sins would come back to haunt him. A slight smile at this memory faded quickly from Asquith's lips; perhaps he had been correct after all. This consumption that was eating his life away may well be his punishment for years of lying, assuming others' identities, and taking what did not belong to him.

At the same time, though, to a certain extent his thievery had been facilitated by others' greed. Asquith had convinced the rich he could make them richer. Their own avarice did them in. And many were willing to pay for the simple pleasure of his company—or at least the company of who they thought he was.

Asquith discovered at an early age that the lemmings of the world would do nearly anything to rub elbows with the high-brow. This was how he made his living; like a fine craftsman, he took pride in his ability to convince others of his importance.

Gazing out the window, he recalled his adventures in India, where he stole his first and only life in self-defense. The native family of the deceased was rumored to have put a curse on him for the killing, one that promised to keep him from finding rest or peace. True, he had not rested much in his career. He had to stay a step ahead of the police, judges, angry victims, and ex-wives. His life had taken him many places: Italy, China, Hong Kong, England, Australia, France, Canada, and of course, his favorite, the United States. Yes, no rest, but his journey had been quite enjoyable all the same.

The mountain countryside he'd spied on the train ride into town reminded him of France, which brought to mind the stone cutter he had met there. The poor old man could no longer hold the tools of his trade, and his vision rendered cutting a straight line difficult. So he put his life's savings into a tavern in a small town in France. Asquith — or Lord Beresford, as he was known at that time—just happened to be hiding out for a week before moving on to new pickings. The old man stayed up late into the night, telling tales of the buildings he had helped construct from lowly local barns to fantastic mansions overseas in America for the rich Vanderbilts. It was there, in the town of Asheville, that the French stone cutter had heard the tales of the Judas coins. He himself had seen the large obelisk dedicated in honor of a leader that sat protectively upon the iron box. The stone cutter was also a Masonic brother and had a cousin who had not only served with Napoleon's Marshal Ney but also met with him in secret in the Americas, where Ney had whispered stories of the coin's existence.

Asquith had heard other tales of the coins as well. One even claimed the talismans were imbued with the power to cure men of their ails and reinvigorate their youth. Tall tales, Asquith had thought. Surely interesting stories to share over good wine, but not possibly true. Yet the older and sicker Asquith became, the more remarkable things he learned in this world, and the more appealing the notion of a health-restoring coin became. But finding the fabled disk, or one like it, was the trick—and precisely what had brought him to Asheville this fall of 1902.

Finally Asquith came upon Mr. Tipton who, as he had been told, would soon arrive at his room. And just then, a knock came rapping at the door. Asquith coughed out a meager, "Come in." His nurse escorted Tipton into the room, and Asquith indicated a dusty, upholstered chair next to the wall by the open window.

"Please sit, Mr. Tipton. Forgive me for not rising, but I am feeling a bit under the weather today. I ask your pardon."

Peter Tipton, a 28-year-old heavyset man with thinning blond hair, sat perched in his chair not knowing what to expect. His legs nearly spilled over the brim of the maroon-cushioned seat. "It's OK, I guess," he replied, with not even the merest idea what this sick old man with the strange accent wanted. The room smelled of dust and cigars. "I was told you would pay me for something."

"I apologize, sir, for the slightest exaggeration. Please let me introduce myself. I am Lord Asquith with Scotland Yard. I believe you have something that belongs to his Majesty King Edward VII of the United Kingdoms of Great Britain and Ireland."

"I ain't got nothing that belongs to no one but me, 'specially no King of England," Tipton defended. He stood, sliding his chair against the wall as if he planned to flee.

"Please sit, Mr. Tipton, and let me explain," Asquith requested. "You see, I know who you are and what you did in April of 1894. Grave robbing, Mr. Tipton, is such a dirty affair, even if it's for someone else."

Tipton sank back into his chair as the color drained from his face. "I don't know what you're talking 'bout."

"Of course you do, Mr. Tipton. Some of King Edward's finest detectives have been investigating this theft."

Tipton glanced towards the door, his first impulse to run and hide as he would have done in his younger days. But he had a family now for whom to provide; he could not just disappear into the country until things quieted down or the strange man left. He thought about attacking, which would be so simple, but the codger's mention of these other detectives had him worried. *Who else knows?* Tipton wondered. He had fooled the Vance family years ago, going so far as to have taken a beating over the whole thing, yet no one knew the truth but him. Even his cousin who had gotten him to help dig up Old Zeb didn't know. Yet today was different somehow. Tipton had not even thought of the coin in several years. Now it all came back to him. And so he peered warily at Asquith and asked, "What is it you want?"

"Why, the coin, of course, my dear boy, and to keep from having to go back to England with you in chains," Asquith replied with a disconcerting smile.

With the shock having passed, Tipton grew a little braver. Narrowing his eyes at his accuser, he fired back, "I thought that thing belonged to the Vance's. They was the last ones to have it."

"Yes. You see, your Mr. Vance obtained it from the original thief and was going to return it but alas, he died before he could. For some ghastly reason, his family buried the coins with him. They were a gift from an Eastern Sultan to Prince Edward VIII when he was born. The same year you appropriated the coins from the good former Governor's grave, they were to be kept as part of the royal treasure and jewels. Their disappearance became an international incident." Asquith drew a shallow breath before continuing. "Your Mr. Vance was good enough to locate the thief when he came to North Carolina to hide, and he recovered the coins. But our hero passed before he could arrange to have the coins returned to the royal family. It was quite easy to deduce that you had taken the missing coin while fulfilling the grieving Mrs. Vance's request to have her beloved husband moved alongside her for eternity. Now, Mr. Tipton, you know you have the coin, I know you have the coin, and my associates know you have the coin. The easiest thing would be to relinquish it and perhaps receive a finder's fee from a grateful King and a friendly country. Or you could be difficult, which would require that I transport you back to England to face a trial and imprisonment."

Thinking he had found his loophole, Tipton replied with a smirk, "You can't do that; I am an American citizen."

"*Tsk-tsk*, Mr. Tipton, please don't think when it comes to matters of international relations one citizen makes much difference in this world."

Tipton was quite familiar with the inner workings of local politics in his own right. He knew if international matters were handled the same way, he had no chance in Hell of winning this fight. He needed an out. "You said something 'bout a reward?"

Even though he was in pain and feeling ill, Asquith derived much enjoyment from this verbal chess match. "Of course, Mr. Tipton. When the coin is returned to England and the King, a proper thank-you will be forthcoming."

Tipton's interest was now piqued. With all the fuss that had been made over the coin when he had taken it, he had hidden it in a safe place. But the thing always nagged at him. It would be good to get rid of it, sort of legal-like, and get paid to boot. "How much?" he asked.

"Mr. Tipton, sir, I won't offend you with talk of money by putting a price on a man's honesty and integrity."

"You're not offending me none," Tipton said simply. "How much?"

"Well, I have been authorized to approve what would be equal to one thousand American dollars," Asquith said, giving the next move to Tipton.

Tipton could have swallowed his tongue. Never did he imagine he would make that much at one time. He could only think to utter, "Deal. I'll be back with it tonight."

"Excellent, Mr. Tipton," Asquith said, clearly pleased with this outcome. "I look forward to your return this evening."

Deciding he had to take the offer before the Englishman changed his mind, Tipton nearly leapt from his chair and went out the door.

Convincing Tipton had been far easier than Asquith had expected. The check mate would be Tipton's return with the object of his desire and if his gamble was correct, Asquith would quickly begin to feel better. Now, he needed to rest. A short nap before Tipton returned would do the trick. Asquith rang the bell on the table, and his nurse came to call. With instructions to awake him upon Tipton's arrival, Asquith lay across the bed with the nurse's assistance. Suddenly there seemed a slight chill in the air. Unbeknownst to him, this was to be his last sleep, as tuberculosis battered the life from him before Tipton returned. The nurse would discover him later that evening.

Meanwhile, Tipton arrived back at the boarding house in time to see his benefactor being taken out the front door on a stretcher and loaded into the back of a wagon before being rolled down Montford Avenue towards town. Tipton saw the nurse standing beside the road, watching the wagon lurch away from the building. He approached the woman to inquire about what had happened.

"Ma'am?" he asked. "You work for Mr. Asquith, don't you?"

"Well, I used to," replied the nurse, wondering at the same moment who was going to pay her and how she would manage to get back to Baltimore.

"What happened?"

"Mr. Asquith passed away not too long after you left," she explained. "He was a very sick man. I hope you had finished your business with him."

"Well, not really," Tipton told her. "Do you know any of the other government men working with Mr. Asquith?"

"Government men? I have no idea what you're talking about. I only know that he came to Asheville after hiring me in Baltimore to work with a doctor who was trying to keep him alive. I have no knowledge of his personal business. Perhaps you could speak to that policeman over there about it." The nurse motioned to a uniformed stocky lad across the way.

"No, that's OK," Tipton said, turning swiftly to leave. Now what was he to do? He had been keeping the cursed coin hidden, failing to profit from it all these years, and now a way he could get rid of it and come out ahead was in the back of a wagon, heading south on Montford Avenue underneath a dirty cotton sheet. What would happen if more English detectives showed up? If Asquith had figured out how to find him, surely others could as well. Worse, they might not be as understanding as Asquith was. Tipton decided he had better put the coin back where he hid it, but it quickly occurred to him that one of those other detectives could have followed him from the boarding house and discovered his hiding place underneath the big rock. He would need to find another spot, keep quiet, and wait to see what would happen. *But where?* If it weren't for his cousin and the idea of quick money for some late-night work, he wouldn't even be in this mess. Tipton should have just walked away when he found out they were going to dig up old Zeb Vance.

That's it! Tipton thought. Hell, since his cousin was the one who got him into this fix to begin with, Tipton might as well give him the coin for the time being—at least until he could figure out how to get his reward. His cousin made and repaired furniture in a shop not far from the public square in town. He had a small tool shed in the back where he kept extra tools and supplies for his business. Tipton had borrowed from the shed before late at night, and he knew how to get in and out with his cousin none the wiser. That's where he would head, taking a circuitous route so the detectives he was sure were shadowing him wouldn't know where he went. That way, they wouldn't be able to swipe the coin from him, cheating him out of his rightful reward.

The sun was down when Tipton crept up on the peeling shed behind his cousin's shop. Certain he had yet to be followed, he found the door to the shed unlocked with the rusted metal padlock hanging on its hasp. Tipton struck a match once he had closed the door behind him. His nostrils flared at the acrid odor of stale turpentine. Careful not to trip and drop his finger-sized lantern, he searched for a place to hide the coin amidst the small stacks of wood and housewares. In the back, on the top shelf, he spied a box with a rope handle and some tools sticking out. It was the tool box his cousin had used when he had had an apprentice working with him in the shop. But the business hadn't turned enough profit to justify hiring another apprentice, so the tool box remained in the shed with extra hammers, small rasps, and saws to be kept out of his way in the main shop. It looked like the box hadn't been moved in years; it was coated with a layer of dust thicker than the fog that rolled off the river. Taking the small tarnished disk from his pocket, Tipton dropped it into the box before placing it back on the shelf.

Tipton was careful not to alert any detectives who might be lurking about as he slipped off the grounds. As he hurried toward the town square, he stopped to glance at the 10-story granite monument in the square's center. He tried to avoid this spot whenever he could. The monument always gave him a strange feeling. In the inky cover of night, that feeling was somehow magnified. He shuddered and quickened his steps down the main drag as he rushed south past Eagle Street, towards home.

The next morning, the local paper carried the story of the passing of Mr. Charles Asquith of England, its ink as fresh as his body. According to news, telegrams were being sent to England in search of Asquith's family to determine to where the body should be shipped. Tipton chose not to return to retrieve the coin until Asquith's final resting place was decided.

A week later, however, there still was no word on what was to become of him. The Noland-Brown Funeral Home on Church Street had been given custody of the body until someone would claim it. Tipton was puzzled by it all. Surely, Scotland Yard would be coming to get their man. Why had they not sent anyone? The papers said he had only 5 dollars in his possession when police searched his belongings, certainly not enough to pay his outstanding bills. Identification and other papers had yet to be located, either. Even more curiously, his nurse could shed no further light on the subject and left town after telegraphing a request for a train ticket home.

Tipton finally figured it out: it was those other foreign detectives. They were here in town watching him, waiting for him to go and get the coin out of hiding. Once he did that, the English authorities would make their presence known and take him back to England along with Asquith's body. Well, they had another thing coming! Tipton would wait them out. Those English police did not know who they were dealing with. He could outlast them easily, and they would have to come pick up Asquith and go back to England without him.

Much to Tipton's surprise, his wait continued into the new year. He noticed as the seasons changed that more and more English detectives were coming into Asheville. They were all mindful not to make the same mistakes Asquith had. None of them gave themselves away with English accents. One or two did have a northern lilt, but these new folk were a careful lot.

Whenever Tipton would go into town, he would notice them staring at him from half-shuttered windows and doorways. Their favorite trick was to watch him in mirrors. So to be on the safe side, he removed all the mirrors in his house. One of the detectives even stopped him on the street one day to ask for directions to the courthouse, but Tipton outsmarted him and ran to hide in a nearby barn until it was safe again. The sneaky bastards even went so far as to bribe his wife and family to spy on him at home. Finally, he was forced to move out of the house and leave them behind in order to protect his life. Even Tipton's cousin, the one who started this whole business, tried to talk to him about why he'd left his family. Tipton quickly realized that his cousin, too, was working against him to try to find out what he had done with the coin. He had to laugh; if only his stupid kinsman knew the coin was in his old shed behind his own store.

Tipton also thought the English police had requested that President Teddy Roosevelt come to Asheville and give a speech a few months after Asquith died. A year later, Tipton could still recall Roosevelt pointing his finger in the crowd and saying, "The government is us. We are the government, you and I." He knew what the President meant: Tipton was a government, and England was going to go to war against him if he did not give the coin back. Well, he would show them all he could take them.

Tipton started doing odd jobs and sleeping anywhere he could to escape the cold and rain: churches, stables, and if he had enough cash, one of the flop houses that could be found around town. While Tipton dozed on the streets, Lord Asquith took up residence in the Noland-Brown Funeral Home on Church Street. No one ever arrived to take custody of the body even though the local mortician, Claude Holder, had taken extra special pride and care in embalming the good Lord Asquith. His skill resulted in such an impressive mummification that people began to visit the funeral home just to see the Englishman dressed in his finest suit, Vandyke beard, and bowler hat. Asquith even acquired a nickname from his admiring public:, The Duke of Asheville, or the "Dook" as the younger crowd called him.

The Duke became so popular among the locals that funeral home employees began to take him out for drives around the public square in a horse and buggy on special occasions. It was on one of these excursions that the Duke and Tipton became reacquainted. Generally, Tipton continued to try his best to stay clear of the square and its monument to the man whose grave he had defiled. Given that the coin was less than a block away from there, the last thing he wanted to do was lead the English detectives who still followed his every move anywhere near its hiding place. The widow in whose barn Tipton had been staying over the last few days had insisted he deliver a basket of eggs and two loaves of freshly made bread to an attorney who had handled a simple property line dispute for her. The only problem was that the attorney's office was squat in the middle of the town square.

Reluctantly and with the utmost care, Tipton went to the attorney's office to make his delivery. Then he accidently ran into a well-dressed gentleman walking down the alley. The gentleman apologized to the disheveled Tipton and asked if he was all right. As Tipton studied this man, he realized he had been trapped. This was one of the English detectives who had come to take him to prison in England. Turning toward the street, Tipton jetted from the sidewalk and ran right into the side of an oak horse-drawn buggy carrying the Duke, who was propped up in the back and being followed by a gaggle of hollering children. Tipton bounced off the side of the buggy so hard, the Duke's stiff corpse slid and leaned over the side as if he was staring down at Tipton.

The black man driving the cart yelled out, "Hey you, watch what you doin' there!"

Tipton spent a few seconds sprawled on his back, mouth agape at Asquith's deathly pallor. Then he regained his footing and ran across the square in hopes of escaping his pursuers. He suddenly found himself facing the fence that encircled the tall gray stone monument at the square's center. He vaulted over it, ran through the crowd back into the street, and stumbled into the path of an electric trolley heading east. He had no time to move. The trolley's steel wheels threatened to slice his feet off at the ankles. He tried to jump backwards but instead fell right in front of the oncoming car, whose engineer could not stop quickly enough to avoid taking off Tipton's head clean at the neck.

Pandemonium erupted in the square as passengers threw themselves from the trolley and men sprinted across the square to get a look at what was going on. The police officer assigned to the square attempted to quell the riot. He shouted to a young onlooker that he needed help from the nearby police station. As the gentleman went off to inform officers of the frightful scene, the policeman took to collecting information from shaking witnesses.

The dead man was determined to be a Peter Tipton, who was known about town to be unstable. Most were not surprised that he would finally crack and go completely mad. A witness described his actions as those of a lunatic, explaining that Tipton had been yelling at the top of his lungs and running into people and things all over the square. Most who knew Tipton expressed their sympathy for his family but agreed it was probably for the best for his wife. This way, she could move on while she was still young enough to remarry and ensure a good life for their son. Tipton's cousin showed up at the square shortly thereafter, as his cabinet shop was not far away, and told the officers that he would accompany them to go break the news to Tipton's wife.

The Duke of Asheville, whose body took far fewer trips around the square following Tipton's untimely demise, was finally claimed in May of 1910 and sent to Washington where he was to be cremated at J.W. Lee Funeral home on Pennsylvania Avenue. From there, the Duke traveled north by airmail to take up residence in a storage room belonging to his last wife's family. Clara, for her part, had since remarried a wealthy businessman, Mr. George Watson of New York and Kingston, Jamaica.

***

The steamship Prinz Joachim of the Hamburg America Line, en route from NY to Kingston, Jamaica: November 22, 1911

Mrs. Clara Pelkey Watson sat beside her sister-in-law, Mrs. Lisa Summerfield, in the dining room of the steamship Prinz Joachim awaiting their dinner mates, Mr. Williams Jennings Bryan, his wife and grandson.

Mrs. Summerfield glanced up to see the Bryans approaching and whispered, "Clara, please try to steer the conversation away from science and religion today. I just can't bear another lecture on the flaws of Darwin and his thoughts on evolution." Clara promised she would as the group took their seats. After dinner, as they waited on coffee and tea, Mr. Bryan looked at Clara and said, "My dear, I apologize for monopolizing most of the conversation during the cruise. We never have gotten around to inquiring about your trip to Kingston. Is it for business or pleasure?"

Clara set her teacup down and reached for the alabaster cloth napkin in her lap, dabbed at the corner of her mouth and replied, "A little of both, perhaps. My husband owns several businesses and a sugar cane plantation in Jamaica, and we are on our way there to join him."

"Oh, most assuredly pleasure, then. Of course seeing your husband is not to be considered business."

Mrs. Bryan gave her husband a sharp glance and hissed, "William!"

Clara was notably amused and responded, "No, not at all. You see, we are also taking home the ashes of my first husband to be buried on the plantation."

Taken somewhat aback by this news, Bryan offered his condolences.

"Thank you, but Charles passed away nearly a decade ago. His remains were only recently discovered."

"I see," stated Bryan, still a little confused. "Your present husband must be very understanding."

"Oh, yes, very much so," Clara agreed. "My first husband spent most of his life traveling around the world and was never really at rest anywhere. The last several years were wasted searching for some silly coin that was supposed to cure his illness. We thought it fitting for him to at last be able to spend eternity at peace on a tropical island."

Bryan struck the top of the dining table with his fist, startling the ladies at the table and making his grandson grin. "That's what I have been talking about; these are not the actions of a species descended from monkeys. You will never see such compassion and caring among the beasts, but only among mankind, the descendants of Adam and Eve. Another proof positive of the fallacy of Darwin's so-called theory of evolution. Why, I tell you—"

Before Bryan could finish the thought, the entire room tumbled to the rear of the dining hall as if to punctuate his point. The sudden quake sent most of the passengers and crew splaying across the deck of the Prinz Joachim. Dishes and crockware came crashing to the floor as an alarm began to shriek.

The ship's chief steward came storming into the dining room and tried to restore order by barking commands to the crew in German and addressing his dining room guests in

English. After some semblance of calm returned to the passengers, the steward set out to see if he should move his charges to life boats and begin abandoning ship. He quickly returned and explained in broken English that the ship had run aground but was not taking on water. The incident was the result of hitting an uncharted sand bar off the coast of a local island. The crew started trying to lighten the ship by offloading unnecessary items and cargo. Once the ship was more buoyant, she would be able to rise off the bar and be backed off the sand to continue on her way to Kingston with little delay.

Unfortunately, some of the cargo deemed unnecessary consisted of items belonging to several of the passengers, including a modest wooden crate containing a brass urn and the ashes of Charles Asquith, the dearly named Duke of Asheville. The crew member who tossed it over the side of the ship stopped to rest momentarily before getting back to lightening the load when he noticed something amiss. The crates being tossed overboard seemed to be floating with the current toward the shore of Samana Island, all except for the last he had tossed out to sea. That one appeared to be drifting away rather than inland with its brethren. He could only shrug and get back to work.

The first attempt to extract the ship from the sandbar was unsuccessful. The next required the removal of the ship's passengers and additional cargo before the ship could be moved. None of the passengers or crew was injured in the incident, and most of the jettisoned cargo was later recovered as it washed ashore onto the beach of Samana Island. But the lone crate housing the last remains of Mrs. Clara Pelkey Watson's husband was never found. It was assumed either to have sunk or floated out to sea to parts unknown. The incident greatly upset Mrs. Watson, who felt she had failed to give her first husband his final rest after all.

Mr. Williams Jennings Bryan would recall easily the love and emotion he had observed on that day while writing the closing summation for the prosecution during the trial of the State of Tennessee vs. John Scopes, which carried a charge of teaching evolution in Tennessee schools. In the closing speech Bryan drafted but never delivered, he stated, "If civilization is to be saved from the wreckage threatened by intelligence not consecrated by love, it must be saved by the moral code of the meek and lowly Nazarene."

Bryan died just five days after losing the trial. He had run for President of the United States three times and served as Secretary of State. For seven years he kept a home in Asheville on the corner of Kimberly and Evelyn Avenues, the house designed by the English Masonic brother Richard Sharp Smith, who was also appointed by Richard Morris Hunt to supervise construction of George Vanderbilt's Biltmore estate. Smith designed Asheville's Masonic temple as well and oversaw its construction downtown on Broadway.

Mr. Bryan's thoughts on the silver coins had been transcribed in a red leather ledger kept in the library of the new Masonic temple. Mr. Bryan never knew of the connection between his traveling companions and the story of the silver coins about which he had read in the ledger started by Zeb Vance, as did many Masons and non-Masons alike who traveled through or resided in Asheville and happened upon the leather-bound volume.

CHAPTER FIVE
Asheville: November 13, 1906

Will Harris had arrived in Asheville yesterday by train and spent the night in one of the flop houses that catered to black men. He swore not to do that again. In order to stay in better style in hopes of shacking up with a lady, Harris decided he would trade in his cash coffers. His years-old boots and tattered shirt might as well be replaced today, too, while he was at it.

Harris felt slightly more at ease in Asheville than he had in Virginia, but he was nevertheless careful not to let down his guard. No one would be looking for him here, though. The thefts and killings in which he had been involved in Charlotte and Virginia were unheard of in Asheville, thankfully.

Harris was an early riser, and the illusion of comfort in the flop house did nothing to encourage him to sleep later than normal. He left before sunrise to prowl the streets downtown on the lookout for any items that might prove useful. Behind a cabinetmaker's furniture repair shop, Harris stumbled upon his opportunity: a shed with a broken padlock, obscured by trees, where Harris could enter without worry of being seen. He slipped through the doorway as quietly as he could, trying to silence the raspy hinges. He tossed aside paint cans, dusty stained rags, and cracked, half-empty bottles of wood stain in search of something of value. Then he spotted a tool box on a far shelf. Maybe if he could work some of the rust off, he could sell what was inside for a little cash. In fact, Harris had seen a pawn shop on South Main across from the intersection of Eagle Street. Surely he could manage to swindle a few bucks for a couple presentable tools and the box itself. He snatched an old oily rag from a nearby chair and set to scrubbing as much grime and rust off the chisels and hammers as he could. After he piled everything back into the box, he set out into a nearby alley to find the pawn shop. Harris knew a black man carrying a tool box in the early morning would be no strange sight, as those who passed him would likely assume he was on the way to a job. By the time he got to the shop, the sun was barely poised over the highest point in town. Harry Finkelstein had just opened his doors. Harris strode to the counter, set the box in front of Harry beside the register, and asked, "What'll ya give me for 'em?"

Finkelstein rifled through the box, silently calculating what each item might be worth and how much he could sell it for if any went unclaimed. He had seen many a man fallen on hard times carrying the tools of his trade for a loan or quick sale. There was nothing unusual about this morning's request.

Finkelstein made an offer that Harris quickly countered before settling on a price for sale. The shopkeeper paid Harris in cash and proceeded with a detailed inspection of the box's contents. The first thing he pulled out was a dingy metal round, seemingly a lone scrap piece from a tool that had once been there. He held it up to the light and called out to Harris, who was busy perusing other items in the shop before leaving. "Sir, did you mean for this to be included in the sale?"

Harris turned to face Finkelstein and squinted at whatever he held in his hand. Harris thought he may as well take it back in case it was worth something; he could still keep his riches from the sale of the rest of the box. "No," he said, lumbering back to the counter. He dropped it into his pocket. "I'd like a rifle and a box of shells."

"OK," Finkelstein replied. "What kind are you looking' for?"

"Something high-powered."

"Got just the thing, Savage 303." He pulled a rifle from the rack behind him and handed it to Harris.

Harris took the rifle and examined it closely, leaning it upon his shoulder and working the action several times. Clearly the man knew a little about shooting. The two agreed on a price for the rifle and two boxes of steel jacketed shells. Armed with his new wares, Harris left the shop to seek out another place that might offer him a new outfit, or at least a fresh pair of boots. It took an hour or two, but soon enough he was outfitted in some cleaner clothes for a fair price. His walking had earned him a drink, he thought, and he settled for a stop at the Buffalo Saloon on South Main Street. He asked for a quart of whiskey, knowing full well the barman was none too pleased at the sight of Harris' rifle. Not wanting to rouse suspicion, Harris decided it would be best to drink and think in private. He found a small wooded area a few blocks away and hunkered down for a sip and a quick doze.

When Harris startled awake some time later, the sun was sinking on the horizon and did little to take the chill from the late autumn air. He sat up and shook some remnants of the overhead tree from his hair. Suddenly he recalled a young lady, the sister of an old acquaintance from another state, who he'd run into the evening before his stay in the flop house. He weighed the options of the flop house against the company of a young woman, and of course the decision all but made itself.

Harris traced his way to the apartment of the girl in question thanks to some tips from generous strangers. Miss Pearl Maxwell lived at the end of Valley Street, near the far corner of Eagle. Harris was more than ready for a hot meal, another drink, and some companionship when he knocked on the door and entered her apartment straightaway as she undid the lock. Expecting to see her boyfriend, Tony Johnson, Pearl was taken aback at the sight of a different man.

It was nearly 11 o'clock that night when a man ran into the Asheville police station at City Hall nearby Ms. Maxwell's apartment. Tony Johnson informed an officer that a crazy brute was trying to kill him and had taken his girlfriend hostage in her apartment, brandishing a large gun. Police Captain John Page and Officer Charles Blackstock responded to Valley Street to investigate. Before they could announce themselves, however, Harris spied their approach through a window and fired point blank through the front door. Officer Blackstock crumpled to the cobblestone in an instant, fatally wounded. Then a second shot through a window struck Captain Page in his right arm.

The intoxicated Harris, thrilled with his perfect shots, accidentally forgot about his hostage and barged out the front door, shouting at the top of his lungs that he was a hound from hell as he jetted down Eagle Street. He nearly stumbled over the two officers he had shot as he tore down the sidewalk. Captain Page gritted his teeth against the hot pain in his arm and struggled to pass his gun to his left hand to fire at the fleeing Harris. As it dawned on Captain Page that his officer was down, he hauled himself to his feet and rushed to the station for backup. He instructed his subordinates to notify Police Chief Bernard of the situation, adding that Officer Blackstock appeared to have been killed. Captain Page reloaded his .38 before he left the station and headed back out into the night. He was determined to stop Will Harris from harming anyone else.

Unfortunately, he was too late. While going up Eagle Street, Harris had been surprised by a sudden open store door on his left. He snapped off a shot in that direction without thinking. The bullet struck and killed the shop owner with a shot to the head. Harris then spotted another man, Walter Corpening, on the opposite side of the street. As he turned the corner and came face-to-face with Harris, he was shot directly in the stomach and bled to death before help arrived. His next victim would be an innocent man sitting on his porch who had the gall to yell at Harris and demand to know why he was shooting. In a matter of mere minutes, Harris had left four dead men in his wake.

Having overheard Harris' fire, Judge Spears Reynolds, who had been visiting the Asheville British American Club on Main Street, drew his pistol. He fired two shaky shots in Harris' direction as he passed by the open door of the club. Both missed, and Harris spun to snap off a shot that lodged in the doorway above the judge's head. Reynolds dropped back to regroup and held his fire. Captain Page rounded the corner at the same time with his pistol now reloaded. He and Harris faced each other across the dark street like duelists from the old West. Both fired yet neither man's shots struck his intended target; Harris because he could barely see in the shrouded darkness save for the flash from Captain Page's firing pistol, and the officer because he was struggling to steady the gun with his weak hand.

Officer James Bailey arrived on the scene moments after at his Captain's orders and attempted to ambush Harris from behind a pole on an adjacent street. He and Captain Page were planted to prevent Harris from entering the open town square. Officer Bailey managed to only strike the roadway near Harris' foot with his shot, due to using a low power 32 caliber revolver not made for distance accuracy. Harris dropped immediately to one knee and sent a steel jacketed rifle bullet up the street striking the lamppost behind which Officer Bailey hid. Passing through the wooden lamppost, the round hit the officer, killing him as he tried to take more careful aim with his small pistol. It went straight through Bailey's head to lodge in a store front across the City Square. Another round struck the Vance monument with such force that it chipped the granite face.

Harris saw Officer Bailey collapse and took off running south toward the train yard. He was certain he had killed several men, but the exact number eluded him. In any case, he knew he needed to hole up for a while and get some rest before considering his next move. Harris was not tired in the least; instead, he was exhilarated. He felt more adrenaline course through him with each downed citizen. *Maybe I am a Hellhound after all,* he thought. Harris stopped briefly to stare into the sky and catch his breath. He heard no footsteps behind him and knew there was probably enough commotion around the dead police officers that no one had followed his direction. He was suddenly overcome by the urge to howl as though he were a triumphant wolf but reined in the impulse lest his cry give away his location.

Harris reached into his pocket to grab more shells to reload his rifle and found the small tarnished disk there instead. He took it out and tried to recall where he had gotten it. Then he remembered it had come from the shed from which he had stolen the tools. He grinned. Perhaps this was a good luck charm. Harris knew of several women in Charlotte who claimed to be witches and made and sold such pieces. One lady, in fact, was related to a man he was later forced to kill. He always wondered if the witch might have put a black spell on him to seek vengeance. What if that shed had actually belonged to a local witch or root doctor? The coin may well have been imbued with some pagan blessing. After all, Harris had never been singularly targeted with as much fire as this evening, yet not one bullet had grazed him. *That must be it,* Harris thought and smiled again as he rubbed the coin between the pads of his fingers before tucking it safely back into his pocket. He never knew when its luck might come in handy.

In the main part of the city, Asheville Police Chief Silas Bernard arrived downtown after receiving a call about the shooting and subsequent deaths of his men. Further interviewing of the gentleman who had first come storming into the police station to report a hostage situation revealed the perpetrator as none other than Will Harris, a wanted criminal out of Charlotte. He had escaped from the prison in Raleigh and was considered a suspect in several robberies and murders across several states. Bernard opted to organize armed parties in hopes of moving in on Harris. Telegrams were sent to other local police departments and county sheriffs detailing the incident, the vagrant's description, and orders to contribute to location efforts.

Within eight hours of the last shot having been fired, Chief Bernard had rounded up hundreds of armed men in the search, with more volunteering as the hunt for Harris continued. The Buncombe County militia was even called to set up a post in the local music hall. But with all local law enforcement tracking the killer, no one was left to police Asheville. There was always the chance Harris could slip past the posse and make his way back into town. Luckily, after two days of searching, an Asheville officer known for his mountain hunting skills tracked Harris to a field in Fletcher, south of the city.

Around noon that same day, Harris was spotted running through a thicket. Bernard's officers and locals gave chase. Harris took several shots at the group, narrowly missing all of them. He took cover in a laurel grove amidst the thick emerald foliage. Men have been known to get lost in the larger thickets that can cover acres of the western North Carolina mountainsides. This thicket, though, was modest enough to be fully surrounded by the two groups of searchers. One of the men in charge called for Harris to surrender. Harris replied with a curse, shaking his fist at the voices outside the brush followed by a shot from his rifle. He plucked up his newfound charm for reassurance. With the coin held snugly in his left hand, he raised the rifle to his shoulder and fired off another round towards his pursuers. Harris hoped that one of the shots would strike a man on the outskirts of the thicket. None seemed to. The energy that had buzzed about him when he made a fatal shot at the earlier men never came. He knew he had to kill again, but he could not see his possible victims well enough to draw a good bead on anyone. If he moved to get a clearer sightline, one of the officers may take an ending shot at him.

Finally, he drew a deep breath and bellowed, "I am Will Harris from Hell and Charlotte! Who will die today?"

Then he heard a command to fire. Over 500 rounds were later estimated to have lashed the thicket, many of which found their way to Harris. His body lay in the center of the bush, riddled with uncountable bullets. A wagon was soon dispatched to carry the body back to Asheville for positive identification. The officer who had found Harris and led the chase to the thicket took initial custody of the corpse and rifle. After Harris was loaded into the back of the wagon, the officer noticed that Harris' hand was fisted over some shiny silver. Prying open his fingers, the officer found what appeared to be a coin, gleaming on one side and dull on the other. He took it from the lifeless hand and put it in his pocket, thinking he would need to give it to Chief Bernard. Harris must have stolen it from someplace during his flight for freedom.

Harris' body was brought back to Asheville to determine if this man was indeed the same Harris on the lam from the Charlotte murders and subsequent prison escape in Raleigh. Witnesses to the shooting identified the body as that of the man who initiated the killing spree on Eagle Street. Law enforcement from Charlotte came in to view the body, until Harris' identity was confirmed to the police chief's satisfaction. Indeed, this man had slaughtered two officers, three Asheville citizens, and possibly many others out of state. The victims in the Asheville massacre were laid to rest shortly thereafter, with Officer Bailey buried in Asheville's Riverside Cemetery and Officer Blackstock in a family plot north of the city. Harris was delivered to the pauper graveyard in west Asheville, overlooking what was to become Patton Avenue.

Some days later, several of the men involved in the manhunt for Harris met at the Asheville Police Department to review the case. John Roebling III, whose father had built the Brooklyn Bridge, was in town visiting at the time of the shooting and had taken up arms to hunt for the murderer.

Buncombe County Sheriff, Henry Reid, city attorney Louis Bourne, Chief Bernard, and Officer Powell who had brought back the body, were all discussing the recent events and how they had affected the community. Bourne advised the Chief, "The Mayor has agreed to reopen the taverns again now that the killer is deceased. He also said he wished to review some ordinance questions next week about alcohol sales to determine if we need to make some changes."

"That's fine, Louis. Just let me know."

Officer Powell recalled the coin he had found in Harris' hand and went to a nearby desk to retrieve it from the drawer. "Chief, I almost forgot to give you this."

"What is it?" Bernard inquired, taking it from his officer.

"A coin I found in Harris' hand after he died in that thicket."

"It looks old," Bernard remarked as he studied it. "Do you think he stole it?"

"Well, no one reported a break-in during the chase. Maybe he brought it with him," Powell answered.

Sheriff Reid reached for the coin, saying, "Let me see it." He had a peculiar look on his face, muttering under his breath, "No, it couldn't be."

"Couldn't be what, Henry?"

"Well, when I was elected, Sheriff Lee came to see me about a week later. Said he needed to tell me something I might find strange. He told me to watch out for any killings involving an old silver coin." Reid shook his head. "He said if I did find the coin, I needed to look at Vance's book. Frankly, I thought that was odd and asked him what it meant. He said he wasn't sure, but the sheriff before him had told him the same thing and he was supposed to pass it along to me... and I guess I'm supposed to tell T.F. Hunter once he's sworn in as the new sheriff. Thing is, I don't recall where he said the book was at."

Intending to pass the token around the room for others to see the Sheriff handed it to Attorney Bourne standing next to him.

Attorney Bourne suddenly seemed uncomfortable. He shifted his weight between his feet and blurted out, "I know where Vance's book is."

Everyone turned towards the attorney as he handed the coin back to Bernard and, without thinking, wiped his palm on his pant leg as if the coin had been covered in something that had rubbed off on his hands.

Chief Bernard stared at him, seemingly concerned. "Louis, what's this about?"

Bourne pulled a rickety chair from beneath one of the windows in the office and sat. He sighed. "See, there were two coins that were put in the care of the Vance family several years ago. First Robert, then Zeb. One was lost or stolen and involved in some sort of murder and hanging in Morganton. But Zeb got it back, and sometime after his death one of the coins disappeared again. To keep the leftover one from going missing, it was stuck in a small metal box beneath the monument on the square. Zeb wrote down in a journal the history of the coins as he knew it, and his brother continued recording after Zeb died, saying that the missing coin was never found and that others should keep a look out for it."

"Where is this book?" Bernard asked.

"In the library in the Masonic Lodge. I've read it myself."

"OK, so what's so special about this coin?"

"It's been rumored to be one of the 30 pieces of silver used to pay Judas for betraying Christ."

"You're kidding," Bernard grunted.

"Well, that's what the book says." Bourne shrugged in response.

"You sure this is the same coin Vance wrote about in his book?" Bernard asked.

"Well, no, I'm just telling you what I read," Bourne told him. "Vance did have sketches of each coin in the book, and Robert Vance marked underneath the drawing which one they put under the monument before it was built."

Chief Bernard scooped up his jacket. "I want to see that book." Directing his next statement at his Officer "let's keep this coin thing under our hats.

"In any case, who would believe it, anyway?" Officer Powell piped up,

The men set out together in the direction of the town square filled with several of the city's electric trolleys towards the Masonic Lodge a block away. They had considered stopping by the monument to check for any signs of the allegedly buried coin, but decided against it for fear of drawing attention.

As a Lodge member, Bourne had a key to the front door. The building was cold due to an ongoing shortage of coal in the city. A delivery clearly hadn't made it there yet. Bourne led his troop into the dusty library and went for a top shelf from which he removed a crimson leather-bound journal and slid it onto a table in the center of the room. Chief Bernard flipped through the pages until he came upon the sketched diagrams of the coins. He took the actual coin from his pocket to compare to the drawing. Bourne fetched a magnifying glass from the cupboard to assist in the Chief's examination.

After a close look, Bernard traded the glass and coin with Roebling, who had a family background in Masonry and great respect for the craft. "They do appear to be the same coin," Roebling concluded, laying the brass-handled magnifying glass down on the desktop. "What do you think, Chief?"

"I'm inclined to agree." Chief Bernard leafed to the front of the book and began to read what the former statesmen had written. There was a short description of the Leeds trial in 1834; the possible involvement of the killer in other homicides, including the death of Frankie Silver; and the hanging of Charlie Silver for the crime. Zeb Vance wrote about how the coins had been passed from keeper to keeper, along with his ideas about the coins' origin and how, during the trial of Tom Dula, Vance had come to believe in their evil power and decided to document accordingly. The last written page, scrawled by Zeb's brother, detailed the burial of the small iron box, the search for the missing coin, and the agreement between head members of the Masonic Lodge to place the remaining coin in Zeb Vance's care by erecting the obelisk in the town square. Finally, Bernard reviewed one brief paragraph noting the installation of an iron fence around the monument, purchased by NYC merchant Macy, after the granite was finished with an emphasis on remaining vigilant for the missing coin. This paragraph was unsigned.

Attorney Bourne glanced at the chief. "Well?"

"Well, what? Two of my officers and three citizens are dead at the hands of a madman. A city and county were under siege for two days. Asheville is changed now. And I'm supposed to believe a devil coin is to blame?" He huffed. "No, Will Harris was evil before he came here. He killed and robbed before; it just ended in our city."

"Chief, I have studied building and engineering all my life," Roebling said, book in hand. "Engineering is based on facts, the laws of nature and physics. How do we explain away that your officers and others shot at Harris, but not one bullet hit until everyone caught up with him in Fairview? Harris killed Officer Blackstock and then shot Captain Page, who'd shot at Harris and missed. Harris struck many people, yet none of your men were able to down him until he hid in that bush."

"So, by your reasoning, why was the posse able to kill him when he was still holding the coin?" Chief Bernard asked. "Where is that logic?"

"Chief, I'm not saying anything about logic at this point. I'm just telling you that every time Harris killed a man, others were shooting at him and they never hit their mark. But we know he didn't kill anyone else after Officer Blackstock, and that's when he was finally shot."

Roebling pointed and continued, "Look at Vance's ledger. For the first murder listed, the killer took the life of that poor boy's father, and when the posse arrived they wanted to kill him but didn't. Instead Leeds was locked up so he couldn't hurt anyone else before the hangman's noose claimed him. Then Vance says Tom Dula survived the Civil War because he took enemy life as a soldier while in the possession of the coin. After the war, he gave the coin to his first love, who killed Dula's lover. But Dula was hanged for it, instead of the woman, because she had the coin."

Chief Bernard, also a lawman who had passed the NC State Bar, worked off facts and physical evidence rather than hearsay. "This is absurd. What about that fiddle the ledger referred to?"

Roebling shrugged. "We don't have enough information to speculate on that. But it does look like Zeb Vance felt those coins were involved with the killings. Zeb was a smart man."

"So... What do you plan to do?"

"Do?" the sheriff asked. "What's there to do? I had a man kill five good people in my city. That man is dead. Apparently he had property on his person stolen from the Vance family or your Masonic organization. That property has been found and returned." He thrummed the table and asked Bourne pointedly, "What do you think?"

"Well..." mumbled the attorney.

"As representatives of the county, don't you agree?" Bernard turned to the other men.

"If it was stolen, it happened way before I took office and the thief must surely be gone now. Not much more we can do," the sheriff admitted.

"I'm not sure about that," Bourne countered.

Roebling added, "Chief, technically the original owner is supposed to be Judas of Ascarote. Catching a sour look from the

Chief of Police, he smiled and continued. "And as a member of the Pennsylvania State Masonic Lodge, I'd be happy to witness the return of this property to its original keepers."

Bernard looked again at the city attorney and commanded, "Take care of it, then. I don't want to hear another word about it."

Before Bourne could reply, Bernard exited the room. The attorney looked around, saying, "I guess I need to make a call or two. What should we do with the coin for the time being?"

Roebling patted Bourne's shoulder and replied, "Don't worry; I'll take care of that. Until then, you might want to put it under lock and key for safekeeping."

CHAPTER SIX
Asheville: May 1909

The popular Magician, Harry Houdini gave a performance at the Asheville City Auditorium for a sold-out crowd on May 12th, 1909. After his performance, several gentlemen affiliated with the Asheville Masonic Mt. Hermon Lodge were invited backstage to meet the revered magician. After some pleasantries, the Masons were shocked to hear Houdini's request to see the Judas coin and Zeb Vance's journal. The illusionist explained that he sometimes traveled in strange circles and listened to whispers about unusual things. The fabled coin, he said, was precisely why he had arranged an Asheville performance. The Masons, up against Houdini's fame, reluctantly agreed to accompany him to the Masonic Lodge where he examined the coin and accompanying ledger.

After his study, Houdini was asked to record his observations in that same journal to expand the coin's written history. He scribbled, *Interesting item and even more interesting story. Thank you.* with a simple signature beneath.

In 1911 Asheville Masonic Mt. Hermon Lodge and Chapter No. 25 of Royal Arch Masons purchased a building lot that would be the site of a new Masonic Temple. It was designed with a first-floor reading room, library, offices, lobby, and dining area. The second and third floors were to be used by different lodges and rites groups in the community. The temple designed by Richard Sharp Smith, designer of many of Asheville's famous structures. Opened four years later. Items housed in the new building included Zeb Vance's journal along with the iron box and coin.

Houdini returned to Asheville in 1914 to stay at the famous Grove Park Inn for some much-needed rest. He again requested to view the coin and ledger. Houdini advised the current guardians of the coin and ledger of an increase of talk surrounding the coin and its legacy in some of the more mysterious circles the Magician had access to. There was discussion of other similar coins and there influence he had heard whispered about. Not completely sold on the coins mystic abilities, he was concerned about the lengths someone who did believe would go to obtain them.

There was an offer from the entertainer to secure the coin himself. In the end, though, the offer was politely declined and so noted in the ledger signed again by Houdini.

Asheville quickly became a favorite destination for the likes of Thomas Edison, Will Rogers, Henry Ford, F. Scott Fitzgerald, and eight U.S. Presidents. All the while, rumors of the coins' existence continued to circulate. Apparently as they were last seen in the Asheville mountains, it brought many curious into Asheville.

Then the world entered into a great war, and Asheville's men took up arms in the conflict. Those who had been born and bred in the community, having never traveled far, suddenly found themselves aboard ships crossing a great ocean on their way to help European allies. Along with these men traveled stories of their homes: descriptions of sunrises over the mountains, legends of the Cherokee people, and tales of mysterious objects and places. Once the war ended in the Allies' victory, a war prize of a German cannon captured by the 321st Army Infantry was put on display before the Vance monument. It would point west down Patton Avenue from 1919 until World

War II, when it was dismantled for its steel to be used in a new fight.

***

Asheville: April 1925

A large crowd had gathered at the Biltmore train station in anticipation of Babe Ruth's arrival in town for an exhibition game. The mass on the platform was so large, it spilled into the station and onto the streets. The teams agents always arrived in town first to marshal up the crowds, and drum up attendance at the exhibition baseball games. The train porter noted that Ruth did not look so good as he went to assume his position beside the coach door.

"Mr. Ruth? You OK, sir?"

"I'm OK, Tommy, just a little train sick. These long rides are hell on your stomach."

"Yes, sir, that's true. You want me to get you off the back of the train and away from the crowd?" the porter asked.

"No, Tommy, ya gotta make the people happy. Else they won't buy tickets. And if they don't buy tickets, yours truly is out of a job." He rose from his seat and went for the door.

All seemed well until Babe Ruth descended the last step onto the train platform. That's when the ball player collapsed as he lifted his hand to wave at the crowd. Some thought it looked like he had been shot. Others in the crowd thought he had merely fainted, but all realized it was more serious as the athlete was whisked away to Saint Joseph Hospital for evaluation. He was hospitalized for five days. Some newspapers reported Babe Ruth had died, while others claimed he was at death's door.

On the third night of his hospital stay, two 13-year-old boys were caught attempting to break into the Masonic Temple on Broadway. They told officers they had planned on locating some magic in the temple to take to Babe Ruth to heal the baseball great and get him back onto the diamond. The representatives of the temple were contacted to respond to the scene, where it was explained to the young men that the Masons possessed no magic powers. Indeed, if the men had, they would have used the magic to help Babe Ruth themselves if they could. No charges were pressed against the young men with the understanding that they would report to the Masonic Temple the next day to repair minor damage to a window.

After the attempted break-in, it was decided that the small steel box would be relocated to someplace safely removed from magic-hunters and legend-seekers. A small committee of Asheville Masonic and community leaders brainstormed various ideas. One suggested putting the box atop Vance's monument, but fear of a lighting strike shattering it in the middle of the night overruled the thought. Then the committee suggested placing the box in an obvious location where it would be secure and heavily monitored—perhaps the foundation of a building. After all, when the pedestal of the Statue of Liberty was completed, several Masons prodded the mortar with silver coins to hold the final block in place.

Around this time, the city of Asheville was in a building boom and constructing a High School on 50 acres near the end of McDowell Street. Douglas Ellington, a Mason, had designed that building and the new city hall. It was he who ultimately identified the box's hiding place. Asheville High School opened on February 5, 1929, with a dedication ceremony in the auditorium. Included as speakers were the Mayor of Asheville; the Superintendent of Asheville City Schools; designer Ellington; Lee H. Edwards, the president of the PTA; the Headmaster of the private Asheville School; and the President of Duke University.

Yet only five of those present, two on stage and three in the audience, were aware of the secret within the new six-sided rotunda. If lines were drawn from each of the six corners to its opposite corner, where the lines crossed in the center of the room, hidden in a most public place yet obvious to everyone if the rotunda were ever disturbed. The location was also documented in the Vance journal, which was then sent to the N.C. Grand Lodge in Raleigh for safekeeping. Seven months after the opening of the new high school the nation was shook by the financial disaster of Black Tuesday when the stock market crashed in September 1929. This forced the closing of the new high school to students and for several years the building stood empty as it was too expensive for the city to operate such a modern building at that time. Students were moved to other locations that were less expensive to operate.

***

In 1932 another person arrived in Asheville following rumors of mystical enlightenment and power that was said to be hid in the Asheville Valley. He was the son of a New England Methodist minister. William Dudley Pelley. He had served with American troops in Siberia during World War I, perhaps it was there he learned of the magic draw of the Asheville area for the first time from fellow solders who called the mountains home. After the war, Pelley worked as a screenwriter with stars such as Lon Chaney. He claimed to have had a metaphysically enlightened experience in 1928, which was documented in a magazine article, "*Seven Minutes in Eternity.*" He described his out-of-body experiences as if he had "died and went to heaven." Thanks to the nation's interest in spiritualism and the occult at that time, Pelley's work was well received—so well, in fact, that he left Hollywood to begin writing about metaphysical and anti-Semitic viewpoints in Asheville N. C. Once in Asheville, Pelley established a correspondence school, Galahad College. He built his college in a building at the corner of Sunset Parkway and Charlotte Street below the famous Grove Park Inn. The curriculum described as "Christian Economics and the search for Spirit Guidance." Pelley also operated a publishing company in a former bank building located in Biltmore Village not far from the main gate of the Vanderbilt's Biltmore Estate. The publishing house he called Galahad Press, and the documents and tracts published under the name of Pelley Publications. One a weekly magazine, the Liberation, in which he espoused his anti-Semitic views and metaphysical ideals. Pelly created a group of likeminded individuals he called "Silver Shirts" copied from Hitler's Brown Shirts in the 1930s. The Silver Shirts, a nationwide organization used Asheville as its main base of operation. In 1936, Pelley himself ran for President under his "Christian Party." Publishing an anti-Semitic view of the world. Later Pelley published a claim that President Roosevelt had covered up the level of the destruction of the Pacific Fleet at Pearl Harbor. These accusations (even though partly correct as history showed), his alliance with Hitler's views, fraud charges and his Fascist publishing activity, was enough to bring him under federal scrutiny. The anti-Roosevelt article about Pearl Harbor, brought charges of eight counts of making false and seditious statements and three additional charges of intent to cause insurrection in the military establishment. Though he searched before his arrest, the rumors of magic and spiritism in the Asheville mountains never materialized. Like the Duke of Asheville, Pelley had heard stories of the coins and their alleged abilities. He even attempted to use this information to gain Adolph Hitler's favor, who was known to be fascinated with spiritualism and powerful religious items. Hitler had in fact funded many search parties throughout the world looking for such pieces. Pelley never managed to rise to Hitler's favored American status and was convicted and imprisoned in a Federal Penitentiary in Indiana in 1942.

***

Meanwhile, the two coins remained separate while hidden in plain sight. The few who knew of their location and existence eventually passed away. The red leather book containing their story was moved to another city, apart from the coins but readily available for anyone to read. Yet no one did.

CHAPTER SEVEN
Asheville: Present day

"The supreme paradox of all thought is the attempt to discover something that thought cannot think." - **Søren Aabye Kierkegaard**

William stood across from Asheville High School on McDowell Street, paying little attention to the rain. He was too focused on the front of the high school building. The security officer walked up the soaked, cracked granite steps to test the heavy oak entrance doors. Seemingly satisfied with their security, he trudged back to his pickup truck to continue his patrol around the 50-acre campus to check other access points. As he turned onto McDowell Street and passed William, hiding beneath the shadowy overhang of a long-deserted restaurant, the officer removed his cap and shook his head much like a shaggy wet dog after a bath. It made William smile.

He glanced down at the collection of plastic soda bottles near his feet: two pair of green two-liter tubes, one with a smaller plastic bottle duct-taped between them. They were already dripping from the downpour. The tops of the bigger bottles were linked by a cotton rope threaded through their necks as a makeshift handle. The larger bottles, were filled with a mixture of gas, liquid soap, and other chemicals. William's friend Tommy called it Appalachian Greek Fire, whatever that meant. The small bottle was not to be touched till last; it contained dry ice. William had seen it before when he had helped unload ice cream for one of the push-cart sellers who worked downtown in the summer. There was no cap on the bottle, leaving room for smoke to spiral up into the wet air. He couldn't figure out why Tommy had likened what was inside the bottle to fire, though; it wasn't hot. Plus, William loved Greek restaurants and always went to the Asheville Greek Festival. He had never seen any fire there. But Tommy told him it was special. He could really go for a gyro right about now, matter of fact...

Hey. William needed to get back on track. He had an important job. Tommy and Jessie had said he was the only one in the whole town who could do it. And he was proud to have been chosen to help his friends. The fact that William had been able to graduate from high school at all was no small feat. Although he had special needs, he had been determined to finish. It took him almost five years, at 20 years old, to finally walk across the stage for his diploma. The whole school had given him a standing ovation. It remained one of the best moments of his life, and Tommy and Jessie promised William that as soon as he completed this job, he'd get the same recognition. William was thrilled at the thought of everyone cheering for him—maybe he'd even get a medal.

At Asheville High, he had heard the stories of a ghost in the big building. Tommy and Jessie had even shown him a video of the ghost, caught by security cameras one morning before school opened. It had also been photographed in the rotunda, they said, and students were afraid to go to school. They told him someone needed to chase the ghost out, but no one was brave enough to do it. William finally boasted that he wasn't afraid of no ghost. He'd scare it out if he knew how.

Inside a Dairy Queen, Tommy, Jessie, and William had sat squished in a booth where they told him he only needed fire and noise to spook the ghost away. "That's what ghosts are afraid of," they said. The slightest whiff of smoke or fire would be enough to expel a spirit from where it rested. William swore he could do this, and he would soon be a hero, having scared off the ghost to make it safe for students to go back to school.

And so William was given bottles of Appalachian Fire to force the ghost out of the building. All he had to do was wait for the security guard to leave, then sneak to the front door of the rotunda, smash the window, and toss the bottles into the middle of the room. The tubes would do the rest. William clutched the rope handles and hustled toward the towering pink granite rotunda, crouched low to the ground. He knew what he had to do; he had visualized it over and over. He would use the small hammer in his back pocket to shatter one of the glass window panes of the front door. Then he would toss the two bottles through the window. Next, he would empty the contents of a small water bottle into the bottle with the dry ice before quickly screwing on the cap. This bottle, with its taped twin green bottles too, would be thrown through the window. William knew he would have to put his hands over his ears because the louder the noise was, the better it would scare off the ghost. And finally, to make sure the ghost was gone, he planned to take a packet of firecrackers, light them, and toss them through the window so they could pop.

William stuck right to the plan. Just as he expected, the dry ice bomb exploded within a minute of being tossed into the rotunda, leaving shards of plastic and liquid in its place. Then he lit a crumpled string of firecrackers with a Bic lighter and tossed those into the room, too. But the rapid *pop! -pop! -pop!* he waited for never came. Instead, a loud *whoosh* filled the room. William was confused. He peeked through the window and saw the entire room ablaze. He could feel the heat from the fire on his face. Something had gone wrong! He had to get help. He turned to run but had barely made it to the bottom of the stone steps before a second explosion went off, as the heat and flames reached the other two containers of fuel, this one even more booming than the first. The fire blew out the rest of the glass on the front door and licked into the damp night. William slipped on the wet grass surrounding the walkway and tumbled to the ground just as the security guard pulled up to the building.

His face smashed into the damp earth, and suddenly rain water was mixing with the blood streaming from his nose. *I let everyone down*, he thought. He could focus on little else until the security guard tugged him upright to ask if he was OK and what he was doing on campus at this time of day. The towering man did not look friendly then; he was backlit by the fire, appearing to have wings of flames. William was so startled that he hid his face in his coat and couldn't muster the courage to respond to the guard's barking questions.

***

Asheville High School: One week later

Brandon James hated work. Especially dirty, dusty work. It was even worse when he wasn't getting paid for it. "Community service," they'd said, but Brandon thought they might as well call it "something for nothing." It was punishment for getting into a fight at the mall. But at least Sergeant Bishop had seen to it that the work would be at Brandon's school. It was better than picking up trash or painting over graffiti in town, although his sister would have liked that. She was the family artist and scholar who could do no wrong, it seemed. She somehow knew everything or was able to find an answer if you asked her to.

Deep down, Brandon was very proud of her. It had been tough for the both of them: no father, and now their mother was sick in the hospital, ravaged by cancer. She was in such pain Brandon found it difficult to visit her at all. But his sister still did, every day. They lived with their aunt who had moved in when their mother fell ill. In a rare moment of vulnerability, Brandon's sister had whispered to him a few days earlier that she was embarrassed but hoped their mom would just die in her sleep so she could escape the pain. Brandon wasn't sure how to feel about that. It was tearing his sister up inside to watch their mother in such agony with no relief in sight. Her art, books, and school were the only things that kept her going. He knew she would go far in the world. No one could say the same for him, though. Brandon would never forget overhearing one of his friend's father at their house one day: "That boy is burger-flippin' bound."

He wasn't sure what that meant, exactly, so he asked his sister about it. She replied that it meant a career working forever in fast food. That was not well received. The comment had pissed Brandon off so much that it had impacted his entire attitude about work and school. Brandon was easy to anger; his fights and time in juvenile court were evidence enough of that. He huffed his frustration as he continued to sweep up the mortar dust and chunks of clay tile that littered the rotunda. *If that stupid kid hadn't tried to burn the school down, I'd probably be picking up trash in the cold.* Brandon smiled at the thought. Maybe this wasn't so bad after all.

Behind him, an older contractor hired by the school, Harry, was pulling up whatever broken tiles were still in place and replacing them with plates similar to what had been there before. He had informed Brandon that the wax that had been used over the years to shine the floor was flammable, which explained the extensive damage from the fire. Harry was using a small pry tool to loosen and remove the cracked slabs. He'd been working towards the center of the room and finally plucked up the last broken tile to toss into his bucket. "Brandon," he called, pointing with his gloved hand. "Can you come sweep and clean this area?"

"Yes, sir." Brandon liked Harry. Harry treated him with respect, not like a criminal. Brandon had even thought about

82

asking him for an after-school job. Harry was really good at tile work and seemed happy to describe to Brandon what he was doing as he did it. It took a while for Brandon to realize that the sneaky old man was actually teaching him as he helped. Brandon was pretty good at cleaning and didn't mind it at all. He figured Sergeant Bishop had been clever in his community service assignment, too. He must have known Brandon and Harry would get along.

As Harry hauled the bucket out a side door of the rotunda, Brandon swept the remaining remnants of cement and tile into a tidy pile. Then he noticed a square area of discoloration in the cement where the last tile had been. The more dust he cleared, the more distinct the spot became. Finally, Brandon bent down and poked it with his finger. *Tap-tap.* The thing sounded like it was hollow and made of metal.

Brandon went to Harry's tool tray and took out a chisel with a narrow tip. He nudged at the side of the square until its top loosened enough to flip open. It was a box. Inside sat a stiff brown lump mottled with mold. Brandon prodded at it with the chisel and eventually realized it was a pouch of some sort, presumably made of dank, dusty leather, with something inside.

Brandon peered around the dim rotunda to ensure no one was watching and slipped the pouch into his pocket. A mere second later, Harry came back into the room. Brandon pointed out the now-empty box enshrined in the cement. Harry looked slightly puzzled at the discovery and tapped the box free with a small hammer from his belt. It was quite small and bore some engraving.

"Bet it's some kind of pipe tobacco keeper," Harry remarked. "Probably belonged to one of the workmen who built the school. Practical joke, I'd say. A couple of guys probably got mad for some reason and took someone's tobacco box, then buried it in the concrete under the tile. Guess they thought they got the last laugh." He stood up from his squatted position and winced as his knees cracked beneath his work pants. "I've found all kinds of things in these buildings, kid. Behind walls and floors. It's not that unusual. Stone workers always put coins and things in mortar while building."

Brandon chewed his lip curiously. "Why?"

"For good luck, mostly."

"Does it work?"

"I doubt it, but it can't hurt none." Harry tossed the dingy metal box in Brandon's direction. "Here, you take it for doing a good job in helping me."

Brandon caught it and turned it over in his hands. His sister might know if it was worth something. Just then the bell rang to signal a class change. His daily hour of community service was over.

Brandon thanked Harry and grabbed his backpack to go on to his next class. He checked his pocket to make sure whatever he'd snatched from the box hadn't fallen out. Brandon smiled to himself. That fight at the mall and resulting community service might not prove useless after all. For some reason, Brandon felt that change was coming and it was going to be good. He couldn't wait to show his sister.

CHAPTER EIGHT
Asheville Mission Hospital: Two weeks later

Lisa hadn't bargained for this. She was young and single with a good job and a bright future with her company. Yet again, she found herself pulled away from her job dealing with issues that weren't her responsibility. She had not planned on assuming a motherly role at this point in her life. But here she was in the hospital, looking after 15-year-old twins and all the complications that accompany them. A week's worth of lost sleep had left her jumpy. She knew her boss was angry that she had to take more time off to deal with the situation, but in reality she had no choice. To make matters worse, her boyfriend had made himself more and more scarce since finding out. Now he couldn't even be bothered to return her messages. Lisa couldn't help but to feel sorry for herself; she missed him and could really use his help in dealing with all this. As quickly as her self-pity ebbed, though, it was consumed by fury.

Screw him, she thought. I don't need him anyway. She was strong like her father and sister. She could do this. She'd been managing just fine for the last two weeks. And when her sister Lynn had been diagnosed with cancer, Lynn was determined that she was going to beat it. At one point, they thought she had. They went out together to Red Lobster to celebrate Lynn's clean scan. That was the first time Lisa's boyfriend met her niece and nephew. Brandon took an immediate dislike to Lisa's boyfriend and wasn't shy about saying so.

Lynn was in remission a mere 10 months before the cancer returned with a vengeance. It spread quickly and the chemo treatments did little to stop it. Lynn was forced to spend more time in the hospital, which meant Lisa had to devote much of her time to Brandon and his sister Hanna. Once it was clear that there was little left to put toward Lynn's fight, she and Lisa made legal arrangements for Lisa to take custody of the twins. The whole ordeal had been tough on Brandon especially, who already held onto anger over having lost his father in a car accident as a child. Now, the fates were taking his mother away from him, too. He coped by getting into trouble and hanging around other wayward kids. Hanna, on the other hand, was the complete opposite. She immersed herself in books and knowledge to dull the pain of watching her mother slip away.

Today, Lisa sat perched in a yellow vinyl chair just outside her sister's ICU room. Lynn had been in significant pain the last few days, and the doctors warned she may not last much longer. Lisa had picked up Hanna from school to bring her to the hospital to visit her mother. Neither of them had been able to get ahold of Brandon. Hanna had been alone in the room with her mother for nearly a half hour when the elevator at the far end of the corridor dinged open. Brandon stood there for a moment, pausing as if to verify it was in fact safe to exit. Just before the doors peeled back to descend to the ground floor, he stepped off. Walking toward his aunt, Brandon braced himself for the inquisition he knew was coming.

"Brandon, where have you been?" Lisa demanded. "I've been calling you for over an hour! It's 4 o'clock. You should have been out of work by two."

Brandon shrugged lamely and replied, "I'm here now."

Lisa shook her head in frustration. "Your mother's getting worse. She's in a lot of pain and you should be here to support her."

Brandon said nothing as he went into his mom's room. Lisa was concerned; something was off. This after she'd just received a glowing report from his school counselor. He had been assisting with repair work at the high school as part of his community service sentence. Brandon appeared to have a knack for tile and masonry work, the counselor said, as he had helped restore the damaged rotunda on campus. He had even been offered an apprenticeship with the older gentleman who had cleaned up much of the mess. Lisa was so pleased to hear positive feedback that she had permitted Brandon to leave school early two days a week to work with the tile mason. He clearly had a talent for the craft and seemed to enjoy it.

This past week, though, Brandon seemed to be returning to his old ways. Lisa had noticed random young men hanging around who she had never met before. She didn't know the boys' families, either. This did not sit well with her at all. Brandon sat in a chair beside his mom's bed and took her hand. He gave his sister a quick smile as she got up and went to sit with Lisa in the waiting area. She knew Brandon preferred to keep his visits with his mother to himself. He whispered to his mom and stroked her hand, not really minding that she couldn't respond. The fact that she could hear him, as evidenced by occasional squeezes of his palm, was enough.

Hanna slumped down next to Lisa in the hallway and untied her paint-splattered sweatshirt from her waist. She rolled it into a ball and clutched it tightly to her chest, hugging it like a teddy bear. Lisa looked over at her and wondered what she was thinking. Hanna just stared straight ahead, silent. Lisa knew she wasn't so great at the parenting thing, but she felt like she had to say something. Finally, she asked, "Do you know what's going on with your brother?"

Hanna buried her chin in her hoodie. "His girlfriend doesn't like him anymore and won't talk to him."

Lisa tucked a strand of Hanna's hair gingerly behind her ear. "Are you OK?"

She turned away. "Mom's going to die now," she said simply. "She hurts all the time. It needs to stop."

"Well, we've talked about that. We all know it's coming. So does your mom."

"No," Hanna replied, her tone surprisingly firm. "It's going to be soon."

Just as Lisa opened her mouth to respond, Brandon exited his mother's room and headed for the elevator without a word. He punched the orange light as soon as he got there and tapped his foot as he waited for the car to ascend.

"Where are you going?" Lisa asked as she jogged toward him.

"Don't know."

"How long will you be out?"

"Not sure."

"Brandon, we need to talk." He looked straight ahead as Lisa continued, "Would you please just answer your phone or text me to let me know you're OK?"

He flipped up his hood as the doors opened. "I guess," was all he said. And he was gone.

Lisa stood for a few seconds in front of the steel door, undecided on what to do. Then, as if on cue, a flood of people rushed into her sister's room. Hanna peered up at Lisa as she hurried past. "Mom's gone now." Lisa couldn't help but fall to her knees and sob as she watched helplessly while the team worked to revive Lynn.

***

Asheville: Biltmore Avenue, 4 hours later

The Harley Davidson Electro Glide rumbled its displeasure at idling at the light. Sergeant Charlie Wilson sat up straight in the bike saddle, trying to banish from his mind the piles of paperwork and reports that needed finishing. It was Asheville's rush hour, and traffic was fairly heavy. Increased traffic meant exercising more caution in operating a motorcycle on city streets. The light changed from red to green. Wilson eased forward by rolling the throttle in sync with the clutch in his left hand, entering the intersection with a throaty rumble from the engine.

Just then, the radio chirped. "Charlie 30, multi-car 10-50 P. I., pedestrian hit. McDowell in front of the high school."

Wilson pushed the transmit switch and spoke into the boom mic connected to his uniform helmet. "Edward, three also in route."

The dispatcher responded mechanically: "10-4, 17:45 hours."

Switching on his blue lights and siren, Wilson wove through the heavy traffic using his lights and siren to request right away not as an excuse to drive fast and dangerously. The sergeant's unit, with the Asheville Police Department patrol division, investigated traffic complaints, serious accidents, and fatalities on the streets of Asheville. Police radio made it sound like this accident was serious, judging from the patrol units already on scene. As he reached McDowell Street, Wilson maneuvered through traffic to the accident. A fire truck and several patrol vehicles were there as he pulled up. Several firemen stood surrounding a blue Nissan four-door, placing a neck collar on the female driver. The windshield was smashed and the vehicle's airbag had been deployed. A patrol officer was huddled off to the side, talking to the driver in between the working firemen. Just to the right of the Nissan in the next southbound lane was a red Ford Focus. It appeared to have been rear-ended by an older tan Camaro behind it. Another patrol officer had what appeared to be the two drivers out of their vehicles, standing on the lawn of the high school. Their licenses were clasped to his uniform in the clip of a cross pen in his shirt pocket. When he saw Wilson, the officer excused himself.

"Your team going to work this?" he asked.

"Yeah, Johnson is on her way," Wilson replied. "Where's the pedestrian hit? Already gone to the hospital?" There was only one ambulance and one injury on scene.

"Well, yeah, that's the problem, Sarge. We can't find them."

"What?"

"According to the driver of the Ford, the light had turned green and the southbound cars started downhill. All of a sudden the blue Sentra hit the brakes and someone allegedly 'flew' over the top of the Nissan. The driver said the person landed directly on their feet behind the Sentra and stood there for a second. Then the red Ford put on her brakes and the Camaro hit her from behind. Driver said she thought the Sentra was on fire because the car looked like it was filling with smoke."

Wilson nodded. "Airbag discharge."

"Yeah, that's what I thought, too. But I talked to a witness behind the rear-ended car who said she saw that the pedestrian had their back to her. The person just started to walk off. When the witness yelled at them to see if they were okay, the pedestrian ran into the apartment complex across the street."

"What's the Camaro say?"

"Nothing," the officer replied. "Only that the Ford bowed up in front of him and he hit them. He's kind of pissed right now. We told him he has a responsibility to keep a safe distance from the car in front of him so he doesn't rear-end someone."

During a break in traffic, Wilson headed for the east side of the road where another patrol officer was talking to an older woman. Wilson figured she had witnessed the accident.

"What have you got?" he asked.

"I'm not sure, Sergeant. This is Mrs. Black. She saw the accident. Ma'am, will you tell the sergeant what you saw?"

The woman wore hospital scrubs and had a green and white ID card on a neck lanyard, indicating she was an employee of the local hospital. The entrance drive was at the stop light where the drivers of the Nissan and Ford had been stopped.

"I was going up McDowell to work in the ER when the light turned green up ahead. There was someone standing at the bus stop on my side of the road. I thought they were waiting for the bus. But then they put their head down and ran across my lane and in front of that red car. It almost looked like they stopped in front of the car on purpose. I guess they were waiting for the light to change and just ran out in front of the red car as it was speeding up."

Wilson asked, "Where did the pedestrian get to?"

"Over the red car."

"They jumped over it?"

"No," the woman said. "The car hit them, they smashed into the windshield, and then kind of rolled over the top of the car. Suddenly they were just standing at the rear of the car in the street. So I pulled over and got out, expecting the person to fall to the ground, but they didn't. They just started walking away. A lady over there—" she pointed across the street "—started yelling at them and they took off running. I went to the red car and started checking out the driver. The airbag had gone off and I tried to stabilize her until the fire and paramedics arrived."

"Was the damage on the car the same as it is now?"

"Oh, yes, and it looked like the person who was hit had pushed the windshield in almost to the steering wheel."

"Did you see where the person went and what they were wearing?"

"They had on dark pants and a dark hooded jacket or sweatshirt pulled over their head. I couldn't tell you if it was a man or a woman, black or white. I thought they might have been running to the hospital because it's so close. But I called a few minutes ago to check, and no one's seen anyone like that in the ER."

"Thanks, ma'am," Wilson said. He motioned to a waiting officer. "Do you think you could provide a written statement?"

As Mrs. Black began to talk to another Police Officer, Sgt. Wilson told a third officer to have forensics process the red Nissan. "Look at this," he said, pointing at some scuff marks on the front bumper. The plastic covering yielded to the pressure of his flashlight, revealing the compressed foam core within. Wilson then shifted his light from the scuff marks up to the dented hood and shattered windshield. The safety glass had cracked like a spider web but remained mostly intact. Moving closer, he pointed out some fibers in the cracks. The roof and trunk lid were badly dented as well.

"She hit something," Wilson said.

Officer Johnson cocked her head curiously. "Sarge, you sure someone walked away from this?"

"We have two witnesses from different points of view that say they did."

"Well, where the hell did they go?"

"Weird things happen after accidents," Wilson explained. "Adrenaline is a hell of a drug. But I guarantee you that when whoever got away finally crashes, they're going to be hurting."

"Just how far do you think they could get doing that much damage to the car?"

"Don't know. See if we can get a K-9 unit to try to do a track. We'll do all we can to locate them in case they're injured. Call ID, too, to photograph the car and collect those fibers on the windshield." He swung his flashlight beam over the glass once more.

"Yes, sir," came the reply.

Once the scene was secure, Wilson walked back to his bike to check the nearby neighborhoods in case the missing pedestrian would be found there. Hopefully a canine track would find them if nothing else could. After a quick once-over, he would go to the hospital to check on the driver who had struck the pedestrian. All business as usual. But intuitively, he couldn't fathom how a person could be hit and do that much damage to a vehicle while still walking—never mind running— away from the scene. Retrieving his driving gloves from his back pocket, Wilson revved his bike and decided something was not quite right with this accident.

CHAPTER NINE
Asheville High School: Three days later

Every time Brandon stopped to consider his next move, he couldn't think straight. He could barely remember the last few days. In fact, he had no memory of where he had been or what he had done since leaving his mother at the hospital. He only recalled a brief phone call from Hanna, telling him their mother had passed away.

He was having a hard time keeping it together. Brandon was sure no one his age had to carry this much on his or her shoulders. It seemed like the world was falling apart around him. Not only was his mother gone, but his girlfriend Karen had sat him down for a talk right around the time his mom's health began to decline. She said she felt uncomfortable around him, adding that she wanted him to stop calling and following her around. She felt like it was time to move on, she had explained gently, because her life was changing in a way that didn't include him. He was at once furious and devastated. His mother hadn't had a choice in leaving him; her disease had taken her against her will. Karen, however, made her own decision—and it was a poor one, in Brandon's opinion, fueled more by her stupid friends' insistence that he was no good for her than by her own doing. If something happened to him, she would be sorry. He was no stranger to the allure of suicide or self-harm. Given all that had happened, putting an end to his misery might be the least he could do.

"Bitch," Brandon muttered under his breath as he passed Karen's locker in the high school corridor.

His surroundings came to him and he wondered how he'd made it to school. Just as he was retracing his steps in his mind, he walked straight into the chest of a towering student. The young man seemed unfazed apart from losing his armload of books in the collision. He bent down to retrieve them from the polished linoleum, tossing out a slightly irked, "Hey, man" in the process.

Brandon had absorbed the brunt of the impact. As he tried to catch his balance, the magnitude of his recent losses pummeled him. He took a flailing swing at his taller peer out of frustration.

"Calm down, man, it ain't nothing. You gotta watch where you're going." The student studied Brandon with some concern. "Hey, you OK?"

Any inkling of sympathy was lost on him as he ran toward the student at full speed, bearing down and lowering his head like a bull. Brandon knocked him to the floor from sheer force. The student's textbooks and a flurry of loose-leaf paper sailed again into the air. The downed student hopped up quickly and came at Brandon ready to fight. A crowd of onlookers had gathered, cheering on the impending scuffle.

The school resource officer caught wind of the commotion and rounded the corner to intervene. He was met by a sea of bodies crowding the hallway, many recording the incident and fight on cell phones, holding them high like periscopes in the large forming crowd. Along with the vice principal and a nearby teacher, the resource officer stepped in to restrain the larger of the two young men and to corral Brandon. A chorus of boos came in response to the students' interrupted entertainment.

Brandon spun around before the officer could lay hands on him and sprinted down the hall. The officer couldn't get through the crowd in time to catch up and used a two-way radio to inform administration that Brandon was off and running, although no one appeared hurt. Brandon leapt down the closest staircase and dodged into an empty classroom to hide. In the back of the room, he crouched down in a corner to draw air into his lungs as the adrenaline buzzed through him.

A passing staff member had seen Brandon duck into the darkened room and used his radio to call the front office. Officer Chuck Clark, another School Resource Officer assigned to Asheville High, left his post to find the classroom. The teacher waiting outside the door told Officer Clark what she had seen.

He was well acquainted with Brandon, having talked with him several times while he helped with the tile work in the rotunda. He found Brandon near the radiator, arms crossed as he leaned against the back wall of the classroom. The officer gave him a once-over to ensure he hadn't been injured in the fight before saying, "Buddy, if you're not hurt, we need to get you to the principal's office."

"Go to hell," Brandon spat back. "You and your '70s porn 'stache can just leave me the ████ alone."

Officer Clark stroked his mustache absentmindedly. It was something of a running joke in the Asheville PD: that his trademark facial accessory would go gray before he did. He studied Brandon for a moment, as if he were trying to determine the best comeback to that remark, and then he began to chuckle.

"That's good," he laughed. The laugh spread to the school staff member standing outside the classroom door. The laughter turning contagious, Brandon looked up at the officer and slightly smiled. Clark continued "Sarge is going to like that one. I don't need to know how you're familiar with the finer points of 1970s porn, but we do need to find out what just happened and what needs to be done about it."

Brandon slunk out from his corner to follow Officer Clark out of the room. Amidst a series of grunts and "Mmm-hmms" in response to the officer's inquiries came a question: "Will I be suspended?"

"I don't think we've got much of a choice there, son," Officer Clark said. "What you need to be concerned with right now is for how long. Listen, I know you got a lot going on, but if you need help, it's out there. Have you been working with a counselor from Mountain Lights?"

Brandon nodded. He had attended a few therapy sessions as part of a counseling and mentoring program offered to students in the Asheville City school district, but he couldn't say it had done much good. He happened to enter the principal's office at the same time that his hallway adversary was leaving. The other student suddenly seemed much taller than before. "Sorry about the misunderstanding," he said to Brandon as he walked past. "You all right?"

"Yeah, man, it's my fault."

The larger student nodded at Brandon saying "It's cool" The tiny women Brandon assumed was the other students mother grabbed the young man by the sleeve and lead him out the Main Office. As soon as the student and his mother were out of sight, Brandon's aunt entered the office. Officer Clark convened with the other resource officer outside the principal's door to discuss the incident. They decided to review the situation with the unit sergeant and school principal to determine the best way to proceed with documenting the incident.

***

Asheville: Church Street, one week later

Even though it was dark, the street light fully illuminated open areas of the avenue. The two young ladies scanned the alley's shadows as they headed in the direction of their car parked at the bottom of the hill. One of the girls, Jessica, held a digital camcorder in one hand and a Gauss meter in the other. Her companion carried an over-the-shoulder equipment bag with a digital thermometer in her right hand and a camera in her left. Jessica raised the Gauss meter up and down as she walked, noting the needle's movement. "This area has the highest EMF readings on the street," she said to Michele. "I think we should concentrate here."

The digital camera Michele was using had been modified for infrared recording by the two girls from instruction gleaned from an internet video. She was busy taking photos of any spot that gave a low digital temperature reading, mostly the front of the gray stone Methodist church and its surrounding shadows. "Let's put out the digital recorder and try to pick up some EVP."

Jessica placed her Gauss meter in Michele's bag and pulled out a small Olympus digital recorder. "This is Jessica and Michele on Church Street," she reported. "We have received high EMF readings on the street and will attempt to collect electronic voice phenomena from this location." She balanced the recorder precariously on top of a yellow fire hydrant.

Michele took a picture of the device and added, "We know there are many displaced souls from the cemetery that was once here. Some in the catacombs of the churches below us may wish to speak to us tonight. Don't be afraid; just give us a sign of your presence." Both girls strained to hear any sound that might be unusual. They hoped the Olympus recorder would pick up noises that would otherwise go unheard. As they listened in the stillness, a voice emerged from the dark: "Do you have identification?"

Startled, the girls turned in the direction of the voice to see a young Asheville police officer standing behind them with a flashlight tucked under his arm. Beside him was an older officer with one hand over his mouth, smothering his laughter.

"Identification?" he repeated.

Both girls reached into their pockets and produced drivers' licenses. "I'm going to run them and check for warrants," the younger officer said to the older.

The second officer approached the pair, still trying to hold back a chuckle. "Hello, Officer Jones," the girls said in unison.

Jessica swatted him on the shoulder, scolding, "That wasn't funny."

Officer Jones smirked. "It was from where I was standing."

"Why do we have to go through this ID crap every time?" Michele asked.

Officer Jones went to click off the digital recorder atop the hydrant. "Training. If you girls don't want to be checked out all the time, you've got to stop hanging out in places like this late at night."

"Well, we could go find a rave somewhere," Jessica countered.

Officer Jones rolled his eyes. "You know what I mean. Your ghost hunting is going to get you girls in trouble someday."

"Hey, we're on public sidewalks and we know not to trespass. Who's the new guy?" Jessica tilted her head toward the younger officer and leaned in toward Officer Jones, whispering, "He's kind of cute."

"Forget it," Officer Jones said. "He has to keep his head on his job right now. That's why we jumped the call. When I heard the description of the suspicious persons, I had him head this way. He needs more training time dealing with unusual people."

"Unusual people?" Jessica echoed.

"Come on, now, ghost hunters on the street aren't exactly an everyday occurrence."

The younger officer returned with their licenses. "No warrant files, just a ton of field interviews. Last one was a week ago at some place called Helen's Bridge." He shrugged at the mention of the allegedly haunted bridge at the top of Sunset Mountain that looked down over Asheville. "I take it you know them."

"Afraid so," Officer Jones replied. "Girls, meet Officer McGee. McGee, meet the girls from G.I.F.T. Give him one of your cards."

Michele reached into her equipment bag and handed a business card to Officer McGee:

G.I.F.T. - GIRLS INVESTIGATING FANTASTIC THINGS:
BABYSITTING, DOG WALKING, CAR WASHING, HOUSE-SITTING, AND PARANORMAL INVESTIGATIONS.

Officer McGee snorted. "All that side work, plus ghost hunting?"

"We prefer 'paranormal investigations'," Jessica chimed in.

"You were up at Helen's Bridge last week?" Officer Jones asked. "I thought you guys were all done with that place."

"I'll have you know our research has narrowed down the date of Helen's death to one of two possible days, last weekend being the potential anniversary," Jessica pointed out.

"We even got photographic evidence of a possible abnormality that night," Michele chirped.

"You girls photographed Helen's ghost?" Officer Jones inquired, somewhat intrigued.

"An aberration," Jessica said.

"Right. So... a ghost?"

"Well, it's more of a mist."

"A ghost mist?" he prodded, not even trying to hide his sarcasm.

"Kind of a blurred mist," Jessica told him. "We're still analyzing it."

Michele scanned through the images on her digital camera and let out an excited squeal. "We got one!" she exclaimed.

Officer Jones walked over to look over her shoulder. "Well, look at that," he said, surprised to see an image on screen. "It's actually something." The image showed what appeared to be a man sitting in the shadows of the Methodist church. "Might not be a ghost, but it's somebody." He glanced over to Officer McGee. "McGee, escort the girls to their car, and I'll go check it out. I bet it's someone sleeping off a drunk."

As Officer Jones set off in the direction of the church, Officer McGee led the girls down to the end of the street where their car waited. "So, you girls really hunt ghosts?" he queried.

Jessica sighed with exasperation and thought for a moment or two before answering. She hated it when other people mocked what she considered to be a valuable endeavor. "We're paranormal investigators," she finally repeated firmly. "We—"

Just as the group was about to reach the girls' car, crackling from Officer McGee's police radio cut Jessica off. "Charlie, 46. Do you still have those girls with you?"

"10-4."

"Hold on to them. We'll need to get statements."

"Did you find something?" Officer McGee asked.

"Yeah, looks it. Their ghost is real fresh. 10-67."

Michele looked at Officer McGee curiously. "What's a 10-67?"

He shook his head, wondering why or if the girls were involved at all, and responded, "Dead body."

Jessica looked up at him wide-eyed. "Are we in trouble?" She thought for a minute and clutched Michele's arm. "Oh, my dad is going to kill us."

CHAPTER TEN
Downtown Asheville: Later the same night

This was Alan's first time; he wasn't sure what to expect. The street lights gave off a strange yellow cast, muting the colors of the parked cars. Occasionally a street light would project a stark white beam that illuminated the objects below. Asheville was in the process of switching out its energy-leeching sodium and mercury lamps for more efficient, cheaper LED lights, which were to blame for the random color variations. Alan had watched the ongoing installation from the top of nearby Beaucatcher Mountain. In the morning fog, the city's light resembled a patchwork quilt.

He drove carefully to where his partner waited. Pulling up to the curb beside her, Alan unlocked the doors so she could slide into the passenger seat. She had short, dark hair and wore a light floral fragrance that perfumed his car. "Not nervous, are you?" she asked.

"Maybe just a little," Alan admitted.

"Well, let's go," the young lady said as she turned up the radio. Alan put the car into drive and pulled into the street. At the College Street intersection, he turned left to head west through downtown Asheville. He kept waiting for his passenger to direct him. When she didn't, he continued to drive west on

College Street through the middle of town. As he merged onto Interstate 240, signs told Alan he was heading into West Asheville.

The only directive he received was, "Keep going straight."

As he began to cross Captain Jeff Bowen Bridge over the French Broad River, a question: "Do you know who Captain Jeff Bowen was?"

Before he could reply that he knew Bowen was an Asheville City firefighter who had sacrificed his life in a fire near the hospital, Alan caught sight of something in his periphery. It was a person standing next to the edge of the bridge in the eastbound lane. Alan knew there wasn't a sidewalk there; the person seemed to be in the roadway. As he pulled even with the figure, he or she jumped over the guardrail toward the river below.

"Holy shit! Did you see that?"

"See what?" Alan's sidekick seemed none too impressed.

"Someone just jumped off of the bridge on the other side!" he insisted.

"Are you sure?"

"What? Yes! Right when I passed them, they went over."

Realizing her driver was in something of a panic, the training officer took the lead and ordered Alan to exit right and enter the West Gate Shopping Complex. The parking lot had a drive entrance that went underneath the bridge and to the river road below. She then contacted dispatch through her radio to request additional units: EMS, fire, and police. Firefighters arrived at the river within 15 minutes to launch a small search boat. Police lights careened around the riverbank as reinforcements poured in from other City Districts. After the search had been ongoing for 45 minutes the Police Lieutenant who had been designated as the Watch Commander and a Patrol

Sergeant in charge of that area of town met with the field training officer and her rookie, both now donning high visibility yellow and orange reflective vests.

"Are you sure you saw someone go over the railing, Kingston?" the Sergent questioned.

"Actually, Sarge, I didn't see it. Alan did."

The sergeant turned away from his officer to ask her trainee, "Just what did you see?"

"A person was standing in the road and then jumped over the side of the bridge, as we got even with them" Alan responded. Training Officer Kingston noted that no matter how many times the rookie told the story, it never changed. Perhaps he really had seen something.

The fire commander came jogging up to the group and said, "We're going to call it for now. The only sign we can find of someone being in the river is where someone must have pulled out a canoe up on this side."

"Could someone survive that fall?" the lieutenant asked, peering at the two bridges overhead that were easily 150 feet above water.

"Doubt it, but I've heard that someone did in the late '80s. Broken all to pieces but lived. So I guess anything's possible."

"Do you think the kid saw someone go over the rail?" the fire commander added. Glancing at the Field Training Officer to her left the Lieutenant detected a slight nod of affirmative from the F.T.O. then continued. "Yea Chief I think he did".

"OK. We'll be back in the morning for a more detailed search in better light. They will show up one way or another."

Officer Kingston turned to her second in command. "Sergeant, rotate someone through the night to keep the scene secure and under watch. Put everyone else back on the street to take care of the backup on calls for service."

"Yes, ma'am," he replied. Then he turned to Alan and said, "Nice first day, huh, rook? Kingston, complete the report and have Junior here write a statement on what he saw and did."

"You got it, Sarge," she replied and indicated that Alan would follow her back to their patrol car to fill out paperwork. They passed two firemen on the way who were reloading their truck with equipment they'd dragged through the river. Seeing the rookie approaching, one of the men winked at his partner and said wryly, "Yeah, it was his first day on the job."

"I heard he moved here from up north somewhere," the other fireman responded.

"Wow, no kidding. That explains it, I guess."

"How do you figure?"

"Well, he must have seen the Jersey Devil sitting on the guardrail and it just flew off as he went by," the instigator quipped.

"Man, don't be stupid," his partner shot back. "Kid didn't see no Jersey Devil. He must have seen that Moth Man. I heard he likes to hang out on bridges."

"What the hell would the Moth Man be doing here in Asheville?"

"Don't you know, man? He's here on vacation. Came for the beer. Everyone knows we're Beer City." Indeed, a slew of craft beer pubs and breweries called Asheville home. They burst out laughing. Alan turned sharply toward the two and suddenly felt a hand on his arm.   "Forget it," Kingston assured him. "It's just give and take. All in fun. Either one of those guys would give their life to save yours without hesitation. Hell, everyone here on the river now for that matter would. We're all brothers and sisters, family takes care of family and picks on each other some as well. Turning back to the patrol car she finished with "you will get your turn, we all do."

***

North Asheville: Beaver Lake, two weeks later

Brian loved the sound of the water on the lake. Sailboats skimmed across the surface as they strove to outdo each other, swerving around red buoys anchored in the water. He was new to the sport and had gotten hooked on it while on an assignment for the local radio station. That was when he'd first met the "Admiral", who was not really an admiral—at least, no one called him that to his face. The Admiral had been a Naval officer of some sort many moons ago but refused to talk about it. And luckily for Brian, he was an excellent instructor.

Brian had learned that in sailboat racing, winning depended on angles. The Admiral called it *tacking*: the art of catching the wind in your sails and moving at an angle to the wind, changing to head in your desired direction. By using the correct tacks, Brian had pulled ahead of the Admiral and the other boats on the water. It was the first time he had been in the lead. But just as he stole a glance right to check the Admiral's distance, everything stopped. It was as if a hand had seized the sailboat from below. Brian wrestled with the joysticks and switches on the radio control unit in an attempt to loosen the small craft from whatever had snagged it. Then it was over. The other model sailboats overtook Brian and a winner was declared.

"Tough break," the Admiral remarked working his own radio controlled small craft back to shore. "Looks like you got hung on some old fishing line. Guess you'll have to go out and get her."

"Yeah, suppose so." Brian was clearly dejected at having had victory snatched away from him.

The model yacht club had access to a small rowboat intended for retrieval of floating course markers and wayward boats that needed assistance. Brian began rowing out to his stranded craft to untangle it so no other unsuspecting boaters would find themselves stuck. Once he pulled up alongside his sailboat, he bent over carefully so as not to capsize the rowboat as he retrieved his own. But it wouldn't budge. Just as the sailboat's bottom lifted from the waves, something sucked it back down. And so Brian pulled harder. The boat sloshed free to reveal what had been holding it: a large black trash bag. He set his tiny boat aside and went to retrieve the soaked bag, muttering, "If I don't get it now, with my luck I'll end up stuck in it again next race." But the bag was heavier than he expected, and apparently not because it was waterlogged.

"Hey, ya need any help?" came a voice from a fellow racer on shore.

"Nah, I got it," Brian yelled back. Being careful not to lose his balance, he managed a better grip on the plastic bag and pulled it up to flip it into the boat. Just then a pale, gaunt hand emerged from the water, seemingly lacing its cold fingers around Brian's wrist. He shook his arm violently before realizing the trash bag held a head attached to body. Shouting toward shore for help, he stood up in the boat too quickly and lost his footing as it lurched to the side and up-ended in the water. He went sprawling into the lake, still clutching the trash bag and whoever was inside.

***

North Asheville: Beaver Lake, Saturday evening

It was Saturday, his day off; that's what pissed him off the most. He had to leave his motorcycle in parts all over the garage floor again. "There goes my ride over the mountains tomorrow," Bishop grumbled. He and a Buncombe County Deputy Sheriff School Resource Officer had been invited to ride with the Blue Knights Police Motorcycle Club in Johnson City, Tennessee on Sunday if the weather held out. Approaching the strobe of police lights in front of him, changing the two lane road to one lane told him he wouldn't be finishing his oil change today. His cell phone had command him to the lake and he attempted to locate a safe place to park amongst all the other emergency vehicles parked helter skelter that forced Merrimon Avenue down to one lane.

The Sergeant immediately recognized one of the officers on scene at Beaver Lake but could not recall the second's name. He hadn't even been able to keep track of all the new recruits flooding the Department in the last year. He snaked through the crowd of first responders until he arrived at the lake shore. "What's going on?" he asked the nearest rookie whom he did know.

"They got a body out of the lake, Sarge. Think it's one of your students."

Sergeant Bishop sucked a straw of air through his teeth. "Got a name?"

"No, I think that's why North wanted you called."

Sergeant Bishop had attempted to reach Lieutenant North by phone on the way in but only got voicemail. Lieutenant North was no more than fifty feet away now, on his phone behind the yellow plastic police tape on the other side of the mass of uniforms. When he saw Bishop, he waved him over.

"Bish, thanks for coming out." Lieutenant North lifted the crime scene tape to allow the sergeant entry.

Bishop shook his head. "It's your crime scene. You want me to contaminate it? Not to mention getting on witness lists."

"Half of North Asheville and their dogs contaminated the scene way before any of us showed up," the lieutenant said. "I need to see if you can identify someone."

Bishop followed his colleague to the side of the lake. Firemen were busy gathering up the equipment they had used to retrieve the body from the water. A young officer with a metal clipboard was pestering them, asking each to spell their name so he could get his death scene report done correctly, documenting everyone who had been on scene.

On the ground lay a plastic body bag. Lieutenant North unzipped it to reveal the corpse inside.

She was a pale, blond young woman. A black plastic trash bag appeared to have been taped around her neck but later torn open. "Crap," Bishop growled.

"You know her?" Lieutenant North inquired.

"Yeah, she's one of the kids at the high school. One of my guys caught her with some weed at a ballgame last year. She used to hang out with the wrong crowd."

"Used to?"

"Mm-hmm. Sometime after the start of the new school year she stopped hanging with the troubled kids. And she wasn't showing up in places she shouldn't be. I got the impression she'd found religion of some sort. Whatever it was, she was a lot happier. She smiled a lot more in the hallway when you'd see her." He raked his hand through his hair and heaved a sigh. "Her name was Karen Cane. Should be about 17. Was set to graduate the end of the year if her grades were OK."

"I need a full name and address," Lieutenant North said, nodding toward the bag on the ground. "She still live with her parents?"

"Last I recall, we only worked with her mother when we charged her. I think she was a nurse at Mission Hospital. What's your guess happened?"

"First thought was a suicide. But it's a little difficult to duct tape a trash bag around your neck and over your head. Not impossible, but unlikely. Why go into the lake? We've got a lot of questions and not too many answers. Do you think she would have committed suicide?"

"I don't recall seeing any indicators," Bishop said, "but I'll ask around and check with the staff at school. Are you thinking homicide?"

Lieutenant North looked around carefully, knowing you couldn't toss out the word in a tourist town without some backlash. "Let's keep an open mind. Foster and Willis are the primaries on the investigation. Give them what you know. They'll have to do a notification and speak with the family."

Bishop hated doing death notifications but knew they were unavoidable. "I'll go with them," he offered.

"No," Lieutenant North replied. "Two detectives and a chaplain are enough of a crowd. We don't want to overwhelm the family."

Bishop knew it was his duty to notify the mother. The lieutenant was right, though; he did need to let school staff know before Monday, two days away. The superintendent and principal especially had to be kept abreast of the situation. If this was a homicide, the media would swarm Asheville High's campus come Monday morning. The school's crisis team was also to be notified to arrange as-needed counseling and interviews with students.

"And what about that fire a couple of weeks ago?" Lieutenant North asked as they walked up the bank. A brisk gust of wind pulsed in line with his steps. "Got that wrapped up?"

Bishop snorted. "Yeah, two rocket scientist seniors convinced a former special needs student that it was up to him to run the school ghost off and provided him with the plan and materials to do so. But they forgot that this guy never lies, and he told the arson investigators the whole story. D.A. has the case now."

"How much damage was done?"

"Lot of scorching and smoke damage. The tile floor of the rotunda got the worst of it and will need some major repair work. We arranged for some of the kids on community service to help with the cleanup. Should have everything open by Tuesday, or at least workable enough that staff and students can get around while the repairs go on. It wasn't like the Catholic Hill School fire, thankfully. Our building was unoccupied and the fire department got there fast."

"Catholic Hill School fire?" Lieutenant North repeated. "Where was that?"

"Oh, sorry," Bishop apologized. "I was helping judge class projects last week. One of the students did a presentation on the history of education in Asheville. The Catholic Hill School was an African American school near Valley Street that caught fire from a furnace issue in 1917. It burned down and killed 8 students and injured several others."

"You're kidding. We had a school burn down in Asheville where children were killed, and I've never heard about it?"

"The history is there, LT, you just have to look for it—or in my case, listen for it," Bishop replied. He pointed behind them. "Did you know that one of the first airfields in Asheville was where the lake is now?"

Lieutenant North rolled his eyes. "Take your teaching hat off, Bishop. You'd better go find Foster and Willis before they leave."

A rookie officer had just finished taking down the names of the firemen and civilians at the scene. His field training officer had to review the notes before he gave them to one of the detectives. "Who's that?" he asked his Field Training Officer, nodding toward a man in a polo with a shoulder holster standing across the grass.

FTO Kevin Ford looked over the top of his glasses at his trainee and answered, "Sergeant Thomas Bishop. He's on the School Resource Officer unit, working in the city schools."

"Oh," he scoffed. "That's him."

"What's that supposed to mean?"

"You know what they say about him, don't you?" "He knows people and things."

"Yes, but the difference is I know what they're talking about," the training officer responded sharply. "You're new. You need to keep your eyes open and your mouth shut more. Sure, Bishop knows people. Almost everyone in Asheville. He's trusted because he's always been fair to everyone. He's always treated them with respect, no matter who they were. And he's been on the force for over 30 years, mostly working with the kids of Asheville in one way or another, as a patrolman, a detective, then a school resource officer. The 'things' people say he knows are those that go bump in the night, if you know what I mean."

The rookie stared blankly, not sure what to think. His trainer gestured emphatically with the clipboard he had been proof reading. "You know, spooky stuff, bump in the night? See, Bishop was always one to listen to people without caring about who they were or what they did. Rest assured Asheville has its share of unusual people and with unusual people comes unusual cases. Any cop will tell you when something happens, people are always calling in with details of their dreams or psychic visions. Police need to look into every tip, even if it's far-fetched. Once a Detective Captain told me he didn't want to have to explain to a family, information wasn't checked out because it came from some astral place and it turned out to be true. Bishop usually got those. So he has most of the insider info on Asheville's weirdest folk. If a local witches group wanted to hold a public ritual, they'd go to Bishop to organize police security."

Ford paused, pushed up his glasses in order to look through them instead of over them, then continued, "They also say that Bishop is a Melungeon. That may be why he thinks that even strange people can be victims of crime and need to be treated with respect. He's been their contact with the legal system. So he's got a reputation for working the weird cases. That's where those jokes come from."

The newer officer was still puzzled. "OK, but what's a Melungeon?"

"Don't they teach anything in college anymore? God. The Melungeon people were here in these mountains way before European settlers showed up. Supposedly where they came from is a mystery. People claim they were descendants from shipwrecked Portuguese sailors around Columbus' time. Or families left behind when Desoto came through here looking for gold. Some link them to the lost colony on Roanoke Island and

Sir Walter Raleigh, or say they're descended from Phoenician explorers who arrived way ahead of Columbus. In any case, they were found living in the mountains of Tennessee and North Carolina when French fur trappers came through the mountains in the early 1650s. But they weren't white, Indian or Black. College types say they're tri-racial. They were called healers, root doctors, blood stoppers... even witches. And they counterfeited silver coins from a silver mine hidden in the mountains. There're lots of legends and stories about them."

"How do you know all that?" the rookie asked.

"Who do you think was my training officer many years ago?" the training officer replied. "Curiosity sent me to the library on my first week on the job to try to answer some questions."

The training officer grinned and added, "Guess nowadays, curiosity sends you to the Internet."

In the midst of all this, Bishop was walking back towards his patrol car. The other Detectives had asked him about a small circle of stones, two feet in diameter, spotted not too far from where the body was found. The Detectives didn't know if there was any connection between the circle and the body, but they were concerned because a similar circle had been chalked on some concrete near a body found a few nights ago on Church Street. That death appeared to be a local who had drunk himself to death. Any connection between the two deaths at this point was purely speculative. At the start of any investigation, anyway, there were always more questions than answers. And in his career, Bishop knew well enough by now that nothing was ever as it seemed. Bishop made a point of stopping and talking briefly to his former trainee and to be introduced to one of the new additions to the Asheville Police Force on his way to his marked patrol car.

CHAPTER ELEVEN
Asheville High School: The next week

Mondays in a high school are always chaotic: a mess of weekend baggage, hangovers, and lingering neighborhood fights coupled with students who'd neglected to take their nurse-dispensed medication since Friday. But this Monday, which brought with it the unexpected death of a student, ushered in a new layer of stress to the student body. School staff members were notified of the event once Sergeant Bishop received confirmation that the girl's family had been given the news.

He was now responsible for locating some of Karen's friends to direct them to the counseling resources available on campus. He also oversaw all the cities School Resource Officers or SROs, many of whom wore several hats: law enforcement representative; pseudo-therapist; liaison between the court system, police, and the school district; and most importantly, a trusted confidant for the students.

Sergeant Bishop and the uniformed officer he has assigned full time to the High School had assisted the detectives with locating friends and acquaintances that had known the victim and were willing to answer questions.

The school day was almost over and there had not been any major issue at any of the city schools Sergeant Bishop and his assigned officers were responsible for. SROs worked to ensure the safety and security of all students and staff on City Schools campuses. Currently there were six full time officers in Asheville City Schools and one-part time officer assisting in the High School. Sergeant Bishop supervised these officers as well as responding to situations himself. This could range from simple damage to property incidents, fights, out of control students, lost children and incidents of weapons on campuses.

Understandably, Karen's death was the talk of the day. Bishop was trying to quiet rumors and quell parents' panic at the thought of their children's safety being threatened. He was used to this in some respects he often found himself fielding calls from parents who were a bit overzealous about reporting so-called "suspicious" activities on campus. Truthfully, he didn't mind these folks because he was more concerned with the parents who seemed not to give a damn.

Karen's preliminary autopsy results indicated that she had suffered blunt force trauma but ultimately asphyxiated from the plastic bag that had been taped over her head. Officials would ask during an upcoming press conference for the public to contact the Investigation unit with any leads. Sergeant Bishop had also received clearance from Lieutenant North to brief the school's superintendent and board members on the information to be released. Apart from the fact that Karen had been on track to graduate in June, there appeared to be no other direct connection as far as the school system was concerned.

However, neither Sergeant Bishop nor the assigned detectives could say for certain that other students were not at risk. The only information he had now that might be worth anything was the fact that Karen may have been associated with a local Wiccan coven. One of her former teachers had remarked that the young woman had seemed to have gotten her act together earlier in the year, which may well have coincided with a new faith-based venture. Although Karen's mother had reported that she assumed her daughter's dabbling in the occult was a phase, she did admit Karen had suddenly become more outgoing and pleasant while at home. Luckily, Bishop's history with such things meant that he knew just where to go to explore the Wiccan scene.

By some strange twist of fate, his phone vibrated just as he was preparing to leave campus for his meeting with the superintendent. His screen lit up with an unfamiliar number and no name, but the message was easily decoded: *2 hours - Coffee - 5 Points - Star*. It had to be from Starla Briggs, the Priestess of a local coven. Bishop had in fact planned to call her to see if she knew anything about Karen. Five Points was a local diner at the intersection of five roads in downtown.

Admittedly, the location of the meeting was a bit unusual. Starla (or Star, as she liked to be called) was a strict vegetarian—so much so that she rarely frequented places that served meat at all. Five Points was your typical family-owned Greek restaurant that just happened to prepare the juiciest burgers in Asheville, plus good coffee and great staff. Bishop ate there often and was well known by the regulars. Even more strangely for Star, Bishop recalled her claiming there was an abundance of negative energy at the place. Not in the restaurant itself, necessarily, but rather the intersection. After the Civil War, five African American Union soldiers had been hanged there following a military trial for suspicion of criminal activity. They were buried in the same spot. Then, in the early 1980s, their long forgotten graves were unearthed during bridge construction. Although they had since been re-interred elsewhere, Star alleged that simply driving through the area drained her and compelled her to avoid the space whenever possible. Fear and concern about crossroads was not unusual. The Blues great Robert Johnson is said to have sold his soul to the Devil at a cross road in Mississippi for his legendary guitar skills in the 1930s.

Bishop figured he had enough time in a two-hour window to make his meeting with the school board before catching up with Star at the diner. As he left the high school in his patrol vehicle, he passed by a female reporter who seemed to be prepping for the ensuing press conference. She caught Bishop's eye as he drove by and turned quickly once she recognized who he was. It was the same reporter Bishop had ordered leave the premises earlier that day when he caught her interviewing unsuspecting students in an unauthorized area about Karen's death. He wondered what exactly would be revealed at the conference, and he hoped that Star could give him some insider info that may shed some light on Karen's passing.

***

Asheville: Five Points restaurant, that same evening

As it turned out, Bishop was over an hour late for this meeting. The school board and superintendent had peppered him with questions for much longer than he had anticipated, and by the time he pulled into the parking lot, it was clear his stomach was set on a burger whether Star liked it or not. She was nowhere to be found when he entered the dining room, so he slid into a red vinyl booth and ordered a coffee to hold him over.

Bishop had sent Star a message letting her know he was at the restaurant. He was on his second cup of coffee complemented by a generous Greek Baklava pastry when she responded with a *Here now*. He replied with a quickly poked "*K*" and groaned inwardly at how technology seemed to be decimating the English language along with nearly everything else. He was instantly reminded of the old paging system that had still been popular back when he first met Star. She had been an EMT on a crew working his area around the same time that he started his police career with the city of Asheville many years ago. Both being first responders from different disciplines, she tended to show up at many of the same scenes to which he was called. She had worked full-time as an EMT while attending night courses at UNC-Asheville. She majored in sociology but was involved with Wicca even back then, and ended up becoming a successful enough author that she left her EMT career to be something of a clairvoyant-writing-research expert.

Bishop looked up as she slipped into the seat across from him and ordered a hot tea. Without a second's hesitation, she said, "I want to talk to you about Karen Cane."

"Was she a member of your group?" Bishop asked, pacing himself with his snack so as not to devour the whole thing before her drink arrived.

"She was," Star answered. She rapped her fingers on the placemat, clearly distracted. "Do you know anything yet? The murder?"

"Who said anything about a murder?"

"Your boss," she said flatly. "I saw the news conference on TV."

"Well, it looks like that's the case, yeah. Someone might have killed her. So what do you know about her? Did she come around often?"

Star stirred a spoonful of honey into her tea and took a long drag, wincing at its heat. "She came to us for the first time about four months ago. She seemed lost, like she wanted direction."

"And you provided it?" Bishop followed, with a lilting inflection that betrayed his curiosity.

"You can knock that off," she spat. "If that's how you want to play this, the conversation's over. Take it or leave it." She slapped a couple bucks onto the tabletop and stood up as if to leave.

"Whoa, all right, I apologize," Bishop said hurriedly. "Go ahead."

Star probably knew it would go this way. The two of them rarely had a serious conversation without Bishop having to cover his ass first. It was a regular ritual between them. "Well, Sarah, one of our coven members, introduced her to me. Didn't think much of her at first. She seemed like just another curious teenager." She blew on her tea and took another sip. "But then, one night after a ritual, she came to me and was asking what I knew about old objects. If I thought an item could make somebody evil."

Bishop raised a brow. "Did she have a spell or something in mind?" he asked.

"No."

"Then why did she think an object could make a person evil?"

"Well, she acted like someone she knew had found something that could do that to a person. Apparently a friend of hers had come upon some talisman somewhere and changed. But not in a good way—the whole situation seemed like it'd spooked her."

"How?"

"She wouldn't say." Star shook her head. "She told me she was concerned, but that was it."

"She didn't say who it was?"

"No, sir. We'd planned to talk about it more, but she's no longer with us."

Bishop leaned back in his seat and stretched. "Do you think... maybe someone killed her over whatever this object was?"

"I don't know. That's your job, isn't it?" Star looked straight at him. "I do know that she was fine until about five days before you found her in the lake."

"Do you know why she would've been at Beaver Lake in the first place?"

"I have no idea."

"But you said she seemed shaken up about this friend and the object?"

"Yes, very much so."

"Why did she think it was evil, you think?"

Star shifted and stirred her tea absentmindedly. "When her friend found whatever it was, they started to do strange things. Bad things. She wouldn't tell me what, though. She just said she was scared."

"Did she say this person was male or female?"

"No. She didn't know much about the object, either. Only that it was small and maybe had something to do with old Masonic symbols."

This admission gave Bishop a start. "Why do you say that?"

Star reached into the folds of her billowy blood-red gown and slid something across the Formica toward him. Bishop stared at it on the table beside his coffee cup. He wanted to reach out and pick it up, but he knew better. It might end up being evidence. He couldn't risk contaminating it.

It looked innocuous enough to the naked eye—just a little metal box with a patina that gave away its age. There were four round metal beads attached to each corner, like stumpy little legs that raised it off the ground. And there were a few splotches of rust and some dimpling, as though someone had tried to pry it open with a tool. Bishop pulled a silver pen from his pocket and spun the box around, managing to lift its hinges with the pen point to peer inside. It looked like a work of origami—like somehow a pair of boxes had been folded and fused together. There was a symbol engraved on its inner hood: a circle around a triangle, with three Ts in the shape of a cross and a few slash marks beside it.

"Do you know what that means?" Bishop pointed with his pen.

"It's called a triple tau," Star replied. "It could be a Masonic symbol, among other things."

"You're familiar with Masonic symbols?" He was surprised.

"They're somewhat similar to Wiccan signs, depending on what they are. Masons and witches believe in helping others. They both hold ritual assemblies. There are commonalities in many such organizations and groups."

"Wait," Bishop said. "So do you know a lot about Masonic issues?"

"My father was a third-generation Mason. I grew up in a Masonic family."

"So what does this mean?" He jabbed toward the engraving again.

"It's a symbol the master Royal Arch Masons used. You can find it on vehicle emblems, rings, and other paraphernalia. Tau is the 19th letter of the Greek alphabet and the last letter of the Hebrew alphabet. The triple tau is actually three taus together. Some say it's supposed to approximate a T and H, to stand for *Templum Hierosolyma*, or the Temple of Jerusalem. Christians interpreted it as Holiness supporting Trinity. In Latin, it's likened to *Clavis ad Thesaurum*, 'a key to the treasure' or 'a place where the precious thing is concealed.'"

"Could it have some other meaning?"

"Of course it could," Star said. "But the point is, whatever gave Karen concern had been in that box."

"But why should she bring it to you?"

"She thought I could find out more about it by looking at it. We were supposed to meet again so I could return it to her, but she never showed up."

"When was that?"

"Just the night before she was found in the lake. Oh," Star added, "and before you ask me, as a person of interest, I was at a lecture at the university that night. That's when we were supposed to meet. Afterward I spent the rest of the evening with friends."

"That's quite the convenient alibi," Bishop remarked.

"Perhaps, but it's not intentional."

"Care to come down to the station and give a statement to a couple of detectives?"

"No need." Star produced several sheets of folded paper from the abyss that was her crimson dress. "Here's my written statement. You've got dates, times, and contact numbers. That should be enough to cover me."

"You know I have to take the metal box with me, too."

"It's yours," Star said quickly. "Take it. It's somehow connected to that poor girl's death. I'd rather not have it around."

"In that case, let me make a quick call." Bishop radioed out for a forensic tech to come secure the box. "But one more thing."

"What else? DNA, just for good measure? You are a pushy sergeant, after all."

"That's just it, actually."

"Oh, excuse me?" Star said. "So, the police department is after witches now?"

"Very funny. It's for your own good. If whoever killed Karen actually touched this thing, they may have left some residue behind. If I have your DNA, and Karen's, they can be eliminated and whatever's left could be linked to the murderer. Unless, of course, that's you."

Star smirked as she submitted without issue, a simple Q-tip swab to the cheek after the forensic tech Ashley Babbit had arrived, Star asked Bishop, "So what do we do now?" after they'd paid Tommy the restaurant owner and returned to their cars. The sun was starting to set, the simple red brick building sat sadly behind them.

"*We* don't do anything. Except wait. I'm just a school cop. There's only so much I can do."

"That's not true, you know. You have a gift, yet you still deny it. You might be more involved with Karen's death than you think. You'll see. Never know what might turn up when you're not looking."

"Any tips?" Bishop inquired.

"I gave you what I've got," Star said. "And it's not like I'm a trusted source, officially speaking. I'm just another Asheville freak, remember?"

CHAPTER TWELVE
Asheville Police Department 100 Court Plaza: East side of the building

It was close to 10 in the evening when Bishop exited the police station after meeting with Lieutenant North and Detectives Foster and Willis. Bonnie Thompson, who supervised the department's civilian Forensic unit, had brought the small metal box in a sealed plastic bag along with a collection of photographs of the victim from the crime scene and at autopsy in Chapel Hill.

"Media will love if there actually is a connection with the occult, not to mention all the Mason conspires stories they could run with" North remarked, himself from a line of Masons. "Bishop, you'll be helping with the investigation since you're in contract with the school district." Bishop had no problem assuming a role in the case considering his long-standing ties to the school system and it was of course the right thing to do. He felt strangely involved with the situation now.

As he headed for his car under a dark cloudy sky, he bumped into the new officer he'd met at Beaver Lake with his former trainee at the start of the investigation.

"Working late, Sergeant?"

"Yes, afraid so," Bishop replied. He noticed the officer was flanked by two other new recruits, who he had seen getting sworn in after they had completed the academy.

Smiling the new officer introduced the sergeant to the other two officers. The taller male officer shook Bishops hand and smiled making the statement, "So you're the department's resident wizard," the taller of the three quipped, extending his hand. The female officer hit the speaker on the shoulder for making the comment. "Hey what was that for? You know this is all David talks about now."

"Oh?" Bishop looked at the officer who he had met at the lake, now obviously uncomfortable at the moment with his friend's statement

Bishop shook his head. "Don't believe everything you hear. People tell all sorts of tall tales and leave out the boring stuff to make them more interesting."

"Well," the tall officer pressed, "They say you're psychic and know when people are lying."

"Wouldn't need anyone else on the force if that were the truth," Bishop laughed. "Wouldn't it help if a cop was psychic? You'll figure out that once you're a cop, you get lied to a lot. Gotta go by body language, not words. You just need to listen and remember what is said ."

"C'mon Sarge, do some psychic magic stuff." Was the reply. This time the Trainee, David struck the taller officer in the shoulder.

Realizing he was cornered Bishop replied, "Do you have a $5 bill on you.?" The taller officer reached into his gym bag and pulled out a wallet taking a bill out and handing it to Bishop. "No, you hold it. Now fold it in two." Bishop instructed. "Hold it in your hand and count to five then put it in my hand." Following instructions, the tall rookie placed the folded bill in Sergeant Bishop's hand.

Bishop's eyes seemed to go out of focus and a strange look over came him. He then started speaking with his voice slightly lower and quieter. "I see you have a need for other people to like and admire you, yet you tend to be critical of yourself." Bishop paused and seemed to be pondering something. "You have some personality weaknesses but are able to compensate for them. I see unused capacity that you have not turned to your advantage. Disciplined and self-controlled on the outside, you tend to be worrisome and insecure on the inside."

Bishop paused again and appeared to be trying to see something off in the in distance that was just out of sight. "At times you have serious doubts as to whether you have made the right decision or done the right thing. You prefer a certain amount of change and variety and become dissatisfied when hemmed in by restrictions and limitations."

"You take pride in the fact that you're an independent thinker; and don't take others' statements without proof, but," pausing again then continuing, "you have found it unwise to be too frank in revealing yourself to others."

"At times extroverted, affable, and sociable, while at other times you are introverted, wary, and reserved. Some of your aspirations tend to be unrealistic." Finished Bishop's eyes came back into focus and he slightly shuddered. The rookie officer looked pale and puzzled.

"Was I correct?" asked the Sergeant.

Appearing slightly shook up the tall rookie said, "Well, yeah how did you do that?"

Shrugging his shoulders Bishop replied, "Well actually I did nothing. Everything I said was a generalization. A Professor by the name of Forer wrote all of that out." "He found that people tend to accept vague personality descriptions, thinking that they only apply to them without realizing that they could fit anyone. It's called the Forer effect."

"P.T. Barnum's fortune tellers did it all the time. It's also called the 'Barnum effect' for that reason. P.T. Barnum had a reputation as a master psychological manipulator."

"Oh Yea, he's the 'sucker born every minute' guy right?" The taller officer replied.

"Actually, he never said that, it was said about him when bought a petrified fake giant" Bishop added.

The younger officer looked puzzled "a what?"

"Never mind, What I said could apply to just about anyone. You decided it applied to you, I didn't. Look it up." See you guy's later, have a good workout." Turning Bishop walked to his vehicle to head home.

The young officer looked at his coworkers and said, "how the hell did he know we're going to work out?"

The female officer turned towards the police department building and replied "you're an idiot look at how you're dressed."

"Oh, yeah."

The three started into the side door when the taller officer in the center stopped suddenly.

"Hey, he still has my $5." The other two officers started laughing and pulled their companion into the side door of the station.

Bishop drove through downtown heading home and stopped in front of the City of Asheville's Civic and Entertainment Center. An older African-American male was playing his saxophone and a younger white male tried to keep up on a beat up accordion. Bishop rolled down his window and hollered out. "hey Tommy." The older black male walked over to the cruiser and leaned in to look on the officer. Bishop handed him the $5.00 bill. "Here you go Tommy, play Misty for me"

Tommy laughed putting the bill in his pocket saying "you got it Bish." The saxophone music started up and the young man joined in on his accordion making for an unusual rendition of Misty. Bishop listened for a bit and thought it was appropriate for downtown Asheville at night. Bishop drove off leaving the buskers, the downtown area and its night life behind.

***

The new Smith Bridge across the French Broad River

At the same time that Bishop was leaving town, Isaac Jeeter walked across the newer concrete of the Smith Bridge, heading east back across the French Broad River. Behind him sat the construction site that marked the old stock yard and the new Brewery. The owl head had been a good sell even if the buyer's identity had surprised him. After all, money was money. The two had plans to meet at the new brewery on Craven Street at 11:00 that night. Isaac knew to watch his back when selling wares, given his father's demise out of carelessness while doing the same. His grandparents had raised him while his mom spent most of her time in prison. As Isaac got older, his grandfather's health declined to the point of dementia, but he still loved to hear the man's stories from the old days—like the one where he learned that his granddad's old 38 caliber revolver had been called an "owl head." Because of the distinct Owl Head relief on the plastic grips of the Iver and Johnson 38 caliber revolver.

Isaac inherited the pistol by default when the old man died. When he received a text message from his customer, wanting to buy a revolver, he'd taken the owl head along with the Raven 25 caliber semiautomatic pistol he carried with him. His plan was to convince his customer that the Raven was a better deal so he could keep the Owl Head for himself. He figured everyone would want an auto nowadays since it was smaller and easier to carry than its stockier brethren. Like always, Isaac had removed the bullets from both guns and kept them in separate plastic sandwich bags in his pockets. It was always smarter to hand a new customer an unloaded gun. That's what set him apart from other sellers: he was smarter than they were. And he stayed away from dealing drugs. Even at 17, Isaac specialized in stolen items: phones, stereos, but mostly guns. He was known on the street as the go-to guy for anything that could shoot. He'd made a name for himself as an accomplished car thief at 11 years old and had even stolen cars for some of the local parts shops looking for hard-to-find items.

He had dropped out of high school as soon as he was able. He figured he was smarter than his teachers, especially since they seemed to know this and picked on him accordingly. No matter; he was probably the richest 17-year-old in Asheville, making more money than they would in a year anyway. And funnily enough, the high school was where he knew his current customer from. Isaac liked to arrive before the buyer, but the buyer had ended up beating him there tonight. Even though they had considered both pistols as Isaac expanded on the pluses of the smaller silver Raven automatic, the buyer seemed set on the old 38. Isaac wasn't one to walk away from a deal and offered a bargain at $100, all profit. Even better, the customer never asked about bullets so Isaac figured he could keep his own and sell them off to someone else later. Now, money in hand, he was headed back to Hillcrest Apartments to spend the night at his aunt's. If not, he'd stay at one of his girlfriend's mother's place instead.

As he crossed the bridge, a scooter pulled up alongside him. He thought nothing of it at first; scooters were prime transportation around these parts, he had sold many himself and if he was lucky enough to know the driver, he might even be able to score a ride to his aunt's apartment to save himself the walk. Even though the traffic light at the end of the bridge was green, the scooter stopped at the far side of the bridge in front of Isaac. He figured it was indeed someone he knew after all. Though when the driver didn't pull over to greet him but instead looped around the bridge again and returned in his direction, Isaac's intuition whispered that perhaps the guy was planning to jack him.

He reached for the gun in his pocket as the scooter closed in on him. And then he did recognize something, although it wasn't the driver's face—it was his grandfather's owl head, pointed in his direction. Just as Isaac tried to shoot one of the scooter's tires, he realized too late that he had neglected to reload the small sliver pistol. His assailant was not so negligent, and a deliberate shot found its way to Isaac's chest.

Looking at the small silver pistol still in his hand he fell to his knees and tried to curse but couldn't get the wanted "mother fucker" out before he coughed and found his mouth full of blood.

Falling over he caught himself with his hands. Isaac tried to breath but found it difficult with an invisible heavy weight on his chest.

Isaacs internal bleeding from his punctured lungs and a clipped artery dulled his senses but he was vaguely aware of the scooter idling nearby behind him. The shooter approached and kicked him in the back of the head. He found himself lying on his face on the cool rough concrete bridge surface. Grabbed by the left foot, he was slowly pulled to the center of the bridge. The road surface cut and tore his face leaving skin and blood on the rough concrete as he was repositioned. Isaac tried to object with a curse but could not, breathing was to difficult. He was slightly aware of a familiar sound. A shaking sound that at first he couldn't place.

Another sound started when the first one stopped, also familiar. A hissing noise. Putting the first noise together with the second he realized his attacker was spray painting on the bridge roadway.

The last thought Isaac had before everything went black was "that son of a bitch is go-na tag me". Then all went black.

***

It was 8:30 in the morning when Bishop arrived at his second crime scene in so many days. The bridge was blocked on both sides of the river. Yellow police tape stretched across the bridge from guardrail to guardrail at both ends, with a second inner line marking the scene's perimeter. Bishop spied a body at the bridge's center. Lieutenant North was already there, waiting for Bishop as he jogged up the roadway.

"Who is it?" Bishop asked.

"Isaac Jeeter," North replied.

"Damn, really? Wonder who he pissed off."

"Don't know, but they sure did a number on him." North ducked under the tape, motioning for Bishop to follow. He handed the SRO Sergeant his phone once they got to his vehicle so Bishop could review the photos. He instantly recognized the victim as a former Asheville High troublemaker. "I gather you believe this is connected to the other investigation," Bishop said.

North swiped through a series of photos and held one up. "What do you think?" This shot was farther away from the body than the others. Isaac's body lay in the middle of the road, his head on the double yellow line. His head was pointed west, his legs straight out and parallel to the line, pointing east towards downtown. A bloody streak across the pavement indicated that someone had gone to great lengths to arrange Isaac's body this way. The young man was also encircled by a sprayed white line. It looked the same as the white gravel circle Bishop had found at the Beaver Lake scene, only in spray paint rather than stones.

North swiped to another shot of what appeared to be a dead older man. He was caucasian, dressed in blue jeans and a flannel shirt. The t-shirt that peeked out from his button-down bore the name of a Myrtle Beach souvenir shop. The man was partially bald with longer hair on the side and a scraggly beard. He was leaning against a gray stone wall with legs outstretched, hands at his sides. He looked to be sleeping with his chin tucked into his chest. To his left sat a 40-ounce brown bottle of beer; on his right, a white circle that had been either drawn or painted on the smooth stone floor upon which he sat.

Bishop glanced at the lieutenant. "What's this? Do I know him?"

"I don't think so," North said. "It's been a long time since he was in the classroom. Name's William, or Billy Martin. He did odd jobs around town for cash. Painting, minor repairs, mowing—that kind of thing. He was a downtown regular in the evening. You might know who found him on the church steps, though."

"Oh. Who?"

"A couple of ghost hunters going around Church Street a couple nights ago. Young ladies."

Bishop perked up. "Jessica and Michelle?" he asked. "Are they involved in this?"

Shaking his head, North responded, "No, don't seem to be. Probably just in the wrong place at the wrong time."

"Cause of death?"

"He may have been poisoned, according to the folks at the medical examiner's office in Chapel Hill. We won't get full tox screens for a week or two. But it looks like somebody put something in his beer."

"Shitty way to die," Bishop grunted. "Could the circles have been there before the body?"

"Yeah, that's what we thought until more white circles started showing up. You know, one is happenstance. Twice is coincidence. Three times, likely to be enemy action."

Bishop pursed his lips. "You think?"

"It's weird, isn't it?" North responded.

"Well, sure, I guess. And what about Isaac? Have you found a weapon yet?"

"Kid had two small sandwich bags in his pocket. One with six 38 caliber rounds, the other with seven 25 caliber bullets."

"Any cash?"

"None."

Bishop sniffed. "That's unusual. Isaac wheeled and dealed like nobody's business. He always had cash on him."

"Robbery could've been a motive, or some kind of payback. The white circle worries me, considering we've seen it more than once now."

"You're not thinking serial killer, are you?" Bishop asked.

"I'm not jumping to any conclusions at this point. But can you think of any links between your student Karen and now Isaac?"

"No, she would've been a freshman when Isaac was still attending. And even when he was at school, he wasn't really at school. He was always cutting class if he even came in at all. So the chance of Karen running into him, much less hanging out with him, is probably slim. The circle thing is weird, though, I agree with you. And whoever's doing it has an eye."

"What do you mean?" North inquired.

"Just look at it." Bishop nodded back toward the scene. "It's perfectly smooth. No starts and stops. Uniform all the way around. This is someone who has practice using a spray can. Maybe even has special nozzles to make a line like that."

"A damn circle is that complicated?"

"Sure," Bishop scoffed. "Try it if you don't believe me. Go buy yourself a couple regular cans and duplicate that circle in a parking lot yourself. See if you can get that same shape without tons of practice. Did you find the paint can?"

"Not yet," North said. "But—" He turned suddenly in the direction of a scuffle a few yards away. Near the yellow tape, Bishop noticed a young African American man—someone who looked like a member of the high school's basketball team—hollering at an officer to let him through. "Do you know that kid?" he asked. "He's gonna start an incident if he keeps yelling at the officer doing scene security".

"Yeah, I'll take care of it," Bishop said. As he made his way to the disturbance, he demanded, "Michael! What's going on here?"

The young man instantly softened when he saw Bishop's face and said, "Officer Bishop, they killed my cousin and no one's doing nothing 'bout it. A cop shot him and now y'all are trying to cover it up."

"Michael, get over here. Let's talk." They huddled out of the way of the other policemen. "How did you find out about Isaac already?"

"Couple of cops and a preacher came to our apartment and told Mom. When I heard where it happened, I came down here to see. Hell, they just gonna let him stay there like that?" He shook his head. "It ain't right, Officer Bishop, it ain't right."

"I know, but this is something that has to be done. Those guys are working for Isaac now. They're making sure they catch whoever did this, and that person will get what's coming to him."

"You just let me know who did it and I'll make sure," Michael snapped, choking back tears.

"You know it's not that simple, bud."

"I know, I know… it's just not fair, Officer Bishop."

"You have any idea who would do this?"

"No." Michael shrugged listlessly.

"When was the last time you saw Isaac?" Bishop asked.

"Yesterday afternoon after practice."

"Did he say anything to you about what might be going on?"

"Naw. He never talked to me about the business," Michael said.

"What type of business was Isaac into now?" Bishop probed.

"He sold stuff. Second-hand stuff."

"*Stolen* stuff?"

"I don't know. He always has some sort of a deal going on."

"He had some bullets in his pocket," Bishop added. "Did he often carry a piece?"

Michael let forth a ragged sigh. "No, he didn't need no gun. No one wanted to hurt him."

"How about cash? Did he owe anybody money?"

"Man, I don't know. Shit. He never would talk business with me. Said he didn't want to get me jammed up at school. He told me I was gonna be in the NBA someday and he'd be my manager, make us both lots of money."

Bishop nodded in agreement. It was probably true; Michael was the best JV player on the team and would have a bright future ahead of him if the odds stayed in his favor. He had basketball and a mother who cared where he was and what he was doing. "Michael," Bishop warned, "someone else may need to talk to you and your mother. If you remember anything, can you just give me a call or come see me?"

Michael promised he would and turned away as one of the EMTs came through with a body bag. Bishop took the young man under his arm. "Isaac is going to be taken to the hospital before he goes to the funeral home. Those guys—" he gestured toward the EMS personnel "are going to do this with as much respect as they can. I need you to make sure everyone else does the same, nodding his head towards the expanding crowd of gathering onlookers. Hey, before I let you go... do you know if Isaac knew any taggers?"

"What?" Michael asked. "Why?"

"Someone had painted the bridge," Bishop said, trying not to lie without breaking confidentiality. "And they might have seen something."

"Don't know, but I'll try to find out."

"Thanks, man. Get outta here and go help your mom. She's gonna need it." As Michael slunk away, something caught Bishops eye as he looked up to the above interstate bridge to his left. Standing on the bridge a figure at the guardrail appeared to be watching from above. Bishop knew there was no sidewalk on that side of the bridge. The person there had to be in traffic, in order to look down. Bishop reached to his belt removing his handheld radio and keyed the microphone and spoke. "150, dispatch"

"Go ahead 150," came the automatic reply.

"Can you have a West district unit check out a suspicious subject on the Captain Jeff Bowen Bridge eastbound and field interview him?"

Officers routinely completed field interviews reports of suspicious people in suspicious places. Years ago this was done by filling out an index card usually kept in the officer's shirt pocket. Today they were completed on a mobile computer. The information can be indexed and searched for investigative purposes.

It appeared to Bishop, the person was looking directly at him. Abruptly the subject disappeared as they moved from the edge of the bridge. Taking up his radio again Bishop spoke to the dispatchers. "Subject has moved away from the edge and may be in traffic at this time. What's the E.T.A. of that unit?"

Wanting a unit on the scene quickly and requesting an estimated time of arrival. He received an answer from the responding officer instead of the dispatcher indicating their arrival. "Adam 32 is 10-23."

Bishop watched from his position below as a uniformed officer appeared on the bridge where the watcher had been just moments before. The officer waved at Bishop and a voice came over the radio on Bishop's belt. "Adam 32 to 150, it's negative no pedestrians on the bridge at all that I can see."

Bishop acknowledged the call and looked towards downtown Asheville. The direction of travel and flow of traffic would've taken them East back towards downtown from the observation point on the bridge. For some reason the observer bothered Bishop, he was not sure why. There was no proof or even any indication the observer was connected to the crime scene below. Yet the observer's presence bothered Bishop. Bishop took the radio and called the officer still standing on the bridge.

"Adam 32, 10 or 15 feet East from where you're standing now do you see anything out of the ordinary?"

"Negative, nothing here other than trash." was the reply.

Bishop started to acknowledge the officer and tell him to go back into service when the officers voice came from radio. "Nothing else but a small white circle and a piece of chalk on top of the rail".

Lieutenant North like all police do, was halfway to listening to the radio traffic and overseeing the final stages of evidence collection when the mention of the circle brought him to full attention. North looked up at the officer on the bridge then towards Bishop. Taking his own two way radio the Detective Lt. directed the Officer to stay on the bridge and sent a member of his forensic team to meet him. Looking back at Sgt. Bishop with a look of apprehension he wondered how far this was all going to go.

CHAPTER THIRTEEN
Asheville High School: The next day

Sgt. Bishop leaned against the cafeteria wall, awaiting the bell signaling the end of lunch and a class change. He always enjoyed lunchtime as a way to observe most of the students at once and ensure nothing funny was going on. Everyone at school seemed to know that he had been assisting with the homicide investigations, and rumors of their potential ties to Asheville High School were spreading like wildfire. Grief counselors had been brought in again; Isaac Jeeter was well known and related to quite a few of the students. Bishop had already been quizzed by students and staff eager to know how close police were to making an arrest in the investigation.

As he wandered along the outer perimeter of the cafeteria, he noticed Denise Miller, a sophomore, approaching him with a smile. He assumed she would have a question about the current cases and was taken aback by her request. "Can I help you, Miss Miller?"

Denise shook her head and replied, "Officer Bishop, I was told to deliver a message to you."

Bishop knew students did not recognize rank and all law enforcement they encountered were referred to as officer in respectful situations. "Is that so?"

"Yes, sir. Granny asked me to tell you to come see her."

Bishop looked at her. "Really?" he asked. "About what?"

"I'm not sure," Denise said. "But she stopped me at the bus stop this morning and told me to tell you."

"Are you or one of your cousins in trouble?"

"Oh, not that I know of," she assured him. Looking around, she continued, "Granny said it was important. You need to see her as soon as possible. She told me to make you promise to stop by today after school. It doesn't matter how late."

"Thank you, Miss Miller. When you see her later, tell her I'll try to come by this evening."

"Thanks, Officer Bishop. You know how Granny is." And did he ever. Granny had moved from the South Carolina low country to Asheville about 20 years ago after a hurricane on the coast had all but wiped out where she lived. She was a Gullah, a direct descendant of Southern slaves. She was also known locally as a root doctor, a sort of fortune teller. He'd be sure to pop over later today to see what the fuss was about.

A legend had followed Granny from the very minute she'd set foot in Asheville. The story goes that a trio of gang members-want-a-bees cornered her at home one afternoon and announced that if she didn't pony up her cash, they would help themselves to whatever they could find. When she challenged them, they made off with her TV, cable box, radio, purse, and a rusty old sword she'd mounted on the wall. Apparently, Granny never filed a police report or spoke a word of the event to anyone. But the next day one of the young men was struck by a car while crossing Merrimon Avenue near the University of Asheville. He died instantly. The young man a few days' later was standing with a group of his peers on a street corner known for illegal pharmaceutical transactions when according to witnesses, the cocked semi-automatic pistol in his back pocket went off all by itself. Whether automatously or accidentally, the 9mm projectile struck his femoral artery causing his peers to scatter and his body to bleed out before first responders could arrive. And then the trios survivor turned up at Granny's door shortly thereafter to return her stolen possessions and save his hide.

Eventually, that same young man got out of the gang community and went off to school, rising to basketball stardom in college in North Carolina. Although street stories were sometimes too far-fetched to be believed, Bishop knew there was usually a grain of truth in them somewhere. He had in fact run into the third assailant, Donnie Washington, sometime later when he serviced Bishops police vehicle at Asheville's fleet garage. He had credited Granny with turning his life around. However, he wasn't keen to say much about the circumstances under which his former friends met their end.

When Bishop met Granny herself for the first time at a celebratory dinner for the city's Parks and Recreation department, she'd sought him out to declare that she knew his great-grandmother. "That's impossible," he'd tried to tell her, considering that his great-grandmother had never traveled more than 50 miles away from the mountain cove in Tennessee where she was born.

Granny had simply reached up to Bishop to put a time-worn hand to his cheek. "Child," she had said, "just study you's head. It'll come to you one day."

That day marked the beginning of many meetings with Granny. Everyone around town came to know her as a community matriarch of sorts who managed to watch over everyone in Asheville. Even Star, the Wiccan priestess, pressed Bishop time and time again for the chance to interview the old woman.

"Soon, soon," Granny had assured him. "It ain't time yet."

Star was never satisfied with that answer. "Can you just ask again the next time you see her?" she always pleaded. But Granny had yet to agree to a meeting.

Before he made sergeant while working in the Detective Division of the Department, Bishop and his late wife had been invited to dinner at Granny's. They were surprised to see other guests in attendance when they arrived: two local pastors and their wives, and a nervous older gentleman who was introduced simply as Mr. Sams. Throughout the evening, the man kept glancing at Bishop as though he expected the plain-clothed detective to pull his pistol and shoot him right there at the table. As the group had begun digging into their dessert, Granny gave Sams a signal upon which he suddenly confessed to having killed a man.

Bishop had tried to interject so he could gather as much information as possible for what amounted to a murder confession for a crime of which he had been totally unaware. Granny quickly hushed him, though, and allowed Sams to continue. The crime had occurred when Sams was but a young man. Once Sams had rambled off the whole story, Granny finally allowed Bishop to call dispatch to arrange a ride back to the station for the man and himself to interview him. Sams did not resist and disclosed a wealth of information once he arrived at the Detective Office.

In 1932, Charlie Sams was 16 years old working for a Mr. Pelly. Pelly, by all accounts, was an unusual man: he operated a small school on Charlotte Street as well as a printing business in Biltmore Village. Sams reported that Pelly had been notoriously superstitious and surrounded himself with like-minded folk. Pelly originally hired Sams to help with building maintenance, deliveries, and various other errands. But the longer Sams worked for Pelly, the more concerned he became with all his talk of the supernatural. Sams turned into little more than a minion who was sent on missions to obscure places to investigate Pelly's wild premonitions. Sams figured he was looking for some sort of buried treasure, and the notion of someday earning a small piece of the loot for himself was the only thing that kept Sams in Pelly's clutches. But the older man grew increasingly frustrated with Sams' apparent inability to track any clues to a worthwhile discovery. Finally, one day he snapped and condemned Sams' soul to Hell in the face of his incompetence.

Although Sams didn't leave that day, he fled from Pelly's shop shortly thereafter when he overheard him speaking with someone in the back room—but when Sams peeked in to see who it was, no one was there. That was enough. He left the job and never came back. But he soon found himself absolutely desperate for money. He decided to rob a local gas station, leave town and eventually send money back to whoever would be the victim as a token of forgiveness. Perhaps unfortunately, the plot did not go as planned. The owner of the local gas station that Sams tried to rob fought back, and Sams shot and killed him with a borrowed pistol. He managed to get out of town before the cops caught onto his trail, and a painter by the name of Gus Langley was later convicted of murdering Russell the station attendant during the holdup. Witnesses had stated that before the robbery, they had seen a car with a New Jersey license plate near the gas station. Police later located a similar-sounding car with a New Jersey plate in Wilmington, 320 miles away. It was driven by Langley, who, although a native of Wilmington, had worked as a house painter in Jersey City for some time. According to trial testimony, investigators had been unable to locate any other car with a New Jersey plate anywhere in North Carolina on the day of the murder.
Other than the license plate, there was absolutely no physical evidence against Langley. The prosecution's case relied mostly on a jail house informant. Langley's cellmate alleged in court that Langley had confessed to the robbery and murder. Although he was eventually sentenced to death, his execution was called off right before its scheduled time due to a clerical error in the judge's paperwork.

Langley was finally exonerated in 1936 after it was proven that he had in fact been hundreds of miles away from the location of the murder on the day it occurred. His conviction was vacated, and he was released after four years on death row. Several times being marched to the death room. His head shaved seven times in preparation for his execution. Langley was granted a total of six reprieves before his finial release. The real killer had never been located until the unusual dinner at Granny's house. Not until that fateful dinner with Granny did the true killer step forward.

And so Bishop would get to work a 55-year-old homicide case, which was certainly new to him. Really, he was always learning something new thanks to Granny. As he drove to her house after school with Denise's urging on his mind, he couldn't help but notice the bright blue trim that framed her otherwise quaint, white-paneled cottage. He had inquired about the seemingly random splash of color some years back, and Granny had informed him that the blue was intended to keep the evil out.

The weather was unseasonably cool that day in Asheville, and he met Granny on her porch where she stood wrapped in a gray woolen shawl to stave off the chill. "Evening, Granny," he said, tipping his cap as he came up the steps. "I was told you wanted to see me." A rickety blue Toyota had passed him on the dirt road as he'd rounded the bend to her home. He asked if his arrival had interrupted a visiting friend.

"No, son, its fine," Granny replied, pulling her wrap tighter around her.

"Anyone I know?" Bishop inquired like someone worried about an older relative.

"Mind to your business, boy, she hissed. That's Mr. Harrison from the store. Poor Man got a boo hag. He stopped by so I could help him out."

Bishop had learned of these so-called "boo hags" through previous conversations with Granny. She described them as evil spirits who could shed their skin at night to become invisible and go anywhere they wanted, even through small cracks and key holes to enter places where they weren't welcome. Other cultures were leery of similar beings, often called a succubus, a Jinn, or just a demon.

"Granny," Bishop warned, putting a hand to his hip. "You know you're not supposed to be doing any doctoring."

"Oh, this ain't no doctoring," she explained. "The boy loves them hot and spicy foods, and those're what attract boo hags. They sit on you chest and cause terrible pain in the evenings. Told him to stop such eating, drink him some buttermilk and some baking soda. That'll run off a boo hag real good."

Bishop shook his head, chuckling. Granny was nothing if not entertaining.

"These killings done got me worried," she noted. "Jack Multer's been showin' himself too much 'round these parts."

Jack Multer was not a person, but rather a low-hanging swamp mist that was often considered a harbinger of things to come. Granny had said before that it was in fact a spirit that took the form of a glowing mist or swath of luminous swamp gas. In fact, Bishop had seen the glowing gas himself while camping with his family near the Dismal Swamp in eastern North Carolina. While the mist was indeed that—a sort of low, wet cloud cover that really came from nature—Bishop had his doubts that it signaled imminent doom. But he wasn't one to challenge the elderly woman's intuition.

"Granny, there's not a swamp near here," Bishop reminded her as he followed her inside into her curtained living room. "Sure you're not just seeing the morning fog from the French Broad River?"

"Jack Multer don't need no swamp when the bad be loose," she said, sinking into an overstuffed chair. "These killings are from somethin' new, but it's very, very old. And it knows you." She leaned forward and pointed a bony finger in Bishop's direction. "It knows yer here. It be comin' for ya."

Bishop was tempted to ignore her. He knew exactly what she meant: something about his Melungeon ancestry. There could be some stock in her idea that whoever had cooked up these murders somehow "knew" him, though. Most of the victims had all crossed his path at some point.

"You needs to take care," Granny told him. She grabbed the Bible that sat on the table between them. A small flannel pouch was tucked between its fragile, dog-eared pages. She held it out. "'Dis gon' protect you."

Bishop accepted the pouch, which was sewn tightly shut. He turned it over in his palm curiously. "What's in it?" he inquired.

"Strong things. Herbs, steel, and powerful Goffer dust." Goffer dust was dirt from a grave, usually that of an important or powerful person. Sometimes it was collected during particular phases of the moon to boost its protective properties.

"Thanks, Granny," Bishop said as he tucked it into his pocket. "Do you know whose dust it is?" He wasn't sure it mattered, but he was interested all the same.

"Sheriff McTeer and Doctor Buzzard," she replied.

The names rang a bell; Bishop had read about Sheriff McTeer from South Carolina. And anyone who knew of McTeer also knew of the root man, Doctor Buzzard, and the rivalry that ran between them in the coastal low country of South Carolina. It was years before the two men became friends. The sheriff had been the youngest ever to serve South Carolina, and he held office for over 38 years. Bishop even had a signed copy of one of his books. He had found it by chance in Fayetteville, NC at a yard sale hosted by the family of a long-retired Army colonel who had passed away. Bishop had been in the area attending classes at the North Carolina Justice Academy and considered it a lucky find.

McTeer was also famous for his study and practice of a form of folk magic called hoodoo, or conjure. He managed to incorporate it into his law enforcement work, and his respect for the occult earned him a unique reputation in his region. Bishop couldn't help but wonder what warranted such powerful protection in his current situation. But before he could ask, Granny had an answer.

"Dis evil know you," she declared. "You been close to it without knowin'. It knows you a good man and can better it in a fair fight. But it don't want no fair fight. It be mocking you with deaths and killings. It knows if yer dead, it can go on doin' it's evil. It fears you stoppin' it."

"But whoever is doing all this is no 'It', Granny," Bishop protested. "There's a person out there who we need to catch before they do any more harm to the people in this town."

Granny's eyes narrowed and she peered sharply at Bishop as though he was the It itself. "You know evil, you seen evil, you fought evil before and mostly won," she said. "You know evil is nothin' but a person who is doing wrong by man, God, or country, who can care but don't. Its only care is that it likes doing what it does. If evil can be in a person, why can't evil be in a thing, too? And a thing is an It."

"Granny," Bishop followed up, exasperated, "do you know who this evil is?" If this meeting was going to be a lesson more than any help, he was going to try to glean whatever information he could from the old lady.

"It knows it's close to ya. It knows you could die with this one. I know 'dis is something you won't believe when you finally see it."

At that, Bishop pulled out his cell phone and scrolled to one of the images of the box Star had brought him. "How about this?"

"I 'spect that's what kept the evil up."

He pressed on. "Granny, have you ever seen something like this before?"

"Not quite," she admitted. "I seen iron pots chained and locked up and was told an evil was trapped inside. And never to touch or open such a thing. Lordy, that was when I was a very,

very small girl." She took a closer look at the photo. "I'll study on it."

That was enough for now. "Well, Granny, I thank you for all this, but I need to go." As she went to rise from her chair, Bishop waved. "No, no, you don't need to show me out."

"Nonsense," she replied, taking his outstretched hand to walk him to the door. She paused near the window before he left. "You have your little witch friend come and see me tomorrow."

Surprised by her forwardness, he gulped, "Ma'am?"

She patted his hand. "It's time, boy. Have her come."

Bishops stood on Granny's porch a moment to gather his thoughts before going to the car. He was nearly at a loss for what to do next. He knew Granny's admissions were important. They meant something; they always did. But what? He wracked his brain for her former premonitions. When a plane crash had killed Bishop's wife, he had been working a sexual assault case. The defendant was killed by the victim's father in a murder-suicide before the trial ended. During the investigation, Bishop had gotten to know the father quite well. This incident, coupled with profound grief over the loss of his beloved wife, was enough to crush him.

Bishop had decided to take a leave of absence from work. Everything he saw reminded him of his deceased wife. He needed to get away and soon found himself in the Badlands of Montana and New Mexico. He couldn't tell if he was looking for answers or just trying to hide. After a month spent hopping between cheap tourist motels, Bishop returned to his makeshift home after losing a staring contest with a nearby mountain. To his surprise, there was a message waiting for him at the motel office. It was from his friend, Granny's grandson, and simply said, "Granny says it's time to come home." Bishop had no clue how she'd found him, and he never had the courage to ask. But he learned never to underestimate her. Even if the answers weren't immediately clear, they would be soon enough after pouring from the mouth of Granny.

CHAPTER FOURTEEN
Asheville: Montford Avenue

Sam was angry; that much was clear. She had stormed out of the old house on Montford Avenue in a huff. She and her girlfriend, Jill, had stumbled upon the aging home almost a year ago and obtained a grant to restore it to its 1800s glory. It became their obsession for the next several months, and when it was finally completed, they moved into it together. Sam's family were devout churchgoers and therefore appalled that the two were together at all, much less living in sin. Since the move, Sam's older brother, Kenny, had been the only person to keep in contact with her.

Sam had recently been offered a counseling job in Raleigh that guaranteed double what she earned as a family therapist in Asheville. But she was reluctant to leave the city. That was why she'd fled the house; Jill and Kenny were intent on talking her into taking the job in Raleigh. Working for a nonprofit may not have paid much, but Sam loved working with local kids and their parents. She didn't want to give that up, and she certainly wasn't in the mood to abandon their precious house on Montford. Jill and Kenny needed to keep their opinions to themselves.

Just as she started down the street, a buzz came from her pocket. *Perfect timing.* It was a student, sounding upset, and

Sam agreed to meet at Montford Park several blocks north of the house. Normally Sam wouldn't agree to after-hours meetings, but this would keep her out of the fire for a little while longer. Today she was all for it.

As she hurried toward the park, she saw the student in the distance. Standing on the other side of the street away from the green park. An older man with a couple of dogs was crossing the street nearby, which could have explained why the student wasn't in the actual park. Sam got closer and noticed the student holding a green 2-liter soda bottle. Sam was puzzling over this when a sound like a muffled pop and flash of light filled the green bottle, literally launching it from the student's hands towards Sam. An instantaneous pain and burning came to Sam's chest. Sam staggered on unsteady feet noticing now that the bottle had seemed to literally fly away. Confused, Sam saw that her appointment was now holding a handgun.

As quick as this realization came the student said simply "sorry Miss Samantha" and the gun coughed out a yellow burst of light. The second bullet hitting her in the side and spinning her around and knocking her to the ground.

Samantha felt a sharp pain in her side and doubled up, clutching at her ribs. The two dogs who had been trotting alongside the older man earlier were suddenly back and barking at the top of their lungs. Sam couldn't perceive much else above the chatter, save for the pounding echo of her assailant fleeing on foot.

***

Asheville: Montford Avenue, four hours later

Bishop arrived on the street to a wash of blue and red lights ricocheting off the homes' windows. Bishop had barely pulled into his driveway when he received the call to come back into town. He lived on the north end of Buncombe County, so it always took a few minutes for him to return to radio range. The mountains blocked much of the Police Departments signal except inside the city limits. Lieutenant North was stationed beside a fire truck, surrounded by a group of uniformed and plain-clothed men and women. He looked more like a coach than a policeman.

Bishop walked up to the huddle. Just then, a lone motorcycle came roaring down an adjacent street with a second vehicle in hot pursuit. The rider pulled short just before the line of caution tape delineating the crime scene and leapt off the bike, helmetless, leaving the motorcycle to lurch sideways onto the street. The person was looking around in a panic as the pursuant car screeched to a halt near the yellow tape barrier. A group of City Firemen leapt from the vehicle sprinting towards the motorcycle rider. Samantha's body was still uncovered and in plain sight in the middle of the sidewalk.

"Kenny," one of the firemen yelled as he ran to stop him from jumping over the police line. Wait! Let them do their job."

Bishop taking in the scene, the flashing lights and the friends trying to calm their brother firemen down. The surrounding drama appearing to Bishop like a scene from a post-apocalyptic movie. Bishop noticed the fire chief was on scene, he walked over to his people to offer assistance in calming his firefighter and brother of the victim down.

Bishop walked to the yellow and black tape. Again he found himself waiting for Lieutenant North to approach him or let him into his crime scene. Suddenly the Police Chief was standing beside him, also waiting for Lieutenant North to approach. Bishop turned the Chief and acknowledged the presence of the tall African American woman with a simple word,

"Boss".

Chief Harding was new to the city of Asheville's Police Department having started less than four months ago. Still trying to find her place in the community and among her officers.

Chief Harding looked at Bishop slightly puzzled and asked "Sergeant why did they call you out? I thought the victim was an older female not one of your students this time."

Bishop shrugged his shoulders, "I'm not exactly sure why I'm here Boss, they call I come".

Lieutenant North arrived at his side of the yellow and black police line tape and acknowledged the two. "Chief, Bishop".

The chief looked at North directly and said "brief me on what's going on"

Lieutenant North brought the Chief of Police up to speed on what was going on behind him. Who the victim was, and her relationship to the firefighter who had arrived on the motorcycle. Apparently regardless of the fire department's best efforts wasn't able to keep him away from the scene.

Asheville Fire Chief Jackson walked up after assisting his firemen into talking the brother, Kenny back to the main station then explaining. "He took one of the guys motorcycles and came out here said he had to just check on his sister. Once we get him calm he said he would go with us to his sister's house to help us talk to her girlfriend. We're still going to have to figure out how to get the motorcycle back to the station," the Chief added.

"If the keys are there I'll see about getting it back." Bishop responded, "I've got a helmet in the trunk of the car, I will need a ride back though."

"Well that solves one problem" the Fire Chief stated.

Police Chief Harding brought the conversation back to the main investigation, "Lieutenant, you said the victim is a counselor of some sort, is she connected to the other killings we've had and the school system?"

"Chief I'm afraid so." was North's answer.

Bishop now interjected, "Lieutenant what was the victim's name again?"

North looked at the yellow legal pad in his hand, "Samantha Harper, she lived on Montford."

Bishop replied, "Crap, she's with the nonprofit group Mountain Lights, they work in the school system, she really cared about the kids and they seemed to like her. Damn."

"What links the other incidents to this one?" Chief Harding asked.

Lieutenant North pulled out his camera phone again and scrolled to an image that appeared to be a photograph of the victim's feet as she lay on the sidewalk. On the sidewalk was a spray-painted white circle.

Lieutenant North said, "it appears the victim stepped into the circle then was killed. "We do have a witness, also looks like an attempt was made to use a homemade silencer made from a 2-liter drink bottle." North continued.

"So we can get a description of the suspect?" inquired the Chief.

"Not much of one, guy walking his dogs said the shooter was wearing dark clothing, a black or dark hoodie with the hood up. He could not tell if it was male-female black or white."

"Have you tried a dog track?"

"No luck," North said. "We'll be canvassing the neighborhood next. Bishop, you reckon there could be links between this victim and any of the others at the school system? Was our other victim being seen by Harper?"

Bishop thought for a moment. "I'm not sure. But I'll find out and get back to you. I'm going to need to contact the school system again. This is really going to shake some trees. Everyone liked Sam."

"I want that information as soon as possible, as much of it as you can tonight and get me written reports on that information ASAP." North added.

Local media had finally arrived on the scene and the number of onlookers outside the police line tape was increasing.

The chief of police looked at Bishop and said," Sergeant go ahead and take that motorcycle back to the fire station and get somebody to bring you back here. Let's try to get that done before the media gets involved in the brother's aspect of the case."

Bishop replied with a "yes ma'am," and headed towards his patrol vehicle to retrieve the helmet he had in his trunk.

Pulling out his cell phone the fire chief looked at the chief of police and stated, "I'll have one of my guy's drive him back here after he delivers the bike."

"Lieutenant," Chief Harding piped up, "is it wise to have our School Resource Unit involved in this investigation? Have you actually tied these murders back to the high school for sure?"

"We have several connections. Bishop's a liaison between the department and the school system, plus he has other resources that could assist with the case."

"What kinds of resources?" Harding countered. "I've heard several stories about your Sergeant since I've been here." She glanced over as Bishop walked away and added apologetically. "None of them negative, mind you, but still stories."

"Well, Bishop does have a lot of connections in the school system and to select groups in the community. It's come in handy for many investigations."

"Right, but I mean this paranormal stuff I keep hearing about. What's going on with that?"

Lieutenant North continued, "Bishop will be the first one to tell you that he has no magical insight, just that he has some useful skills in talking to people. He will admit to being a Melungeon, with his family history going back many generations to the mountains of Tennessee. "Know who the Melungeon people are Chief?"

"As a matter of fact, I am very familiar with Tri- Racial groups and issues. I had a roommate at U. T. who was Tri-Racial. She was part of a Melungeon DNA study when we were at the University."

Lieutenant North was a little disappointed. He liked explaining to others Bishops unique ancestry when it came up. Not given the opportunity to do so this time, he changed directions slightly with his explanation. "Do you know the writer Laura Grant?"

The chief of police looked puzzled at the out of place question and replied. "The romance novelist? I read her books in college."

Lieutenant North smiled, "you mean his books" was the reply.

"Wait, you're saying Sergeant Bishop wrote those books under a pen name?"

"No, it was his brother, Mike. Apparently with the publishing of his first book his publisher thought the books would be better received if they used a female named author." The lieutenant continued, "that was how Bishop met his late wife, she was an artist working on book covers and doing illustrations for novels and children books. Bishop's brother introduced them."

Nodding the chief added, "yes I understand she died in a car accident." The Chief added.

"Not a car accident." Lieutenant North continued. "In the 50s a B-17 bomber crashed in the mountains near here in Haywood County. Conspiracy types suggest it was under strange circumstances. Mike, Bishop's brother was working on a story involving the crash. Mike, Bishops wife and their daughter Sherry, flew over of the crash site in Mike's plane. Bishop's wife Angela, taking pictures to help on the cover design. Their daughter went along because she loved to fly with her uncle, a very experienced pilot and flight instructor." Lt North paused a moment before continuing to explain. "The small plane crashed not far from the site of the B-17 crash site. Bishop was a detective at the time. He inherited Mike's estate, book royalties and movie rights to two of the books." Shrugging his shoulders North added, "Bishop doesn't need to

155

work; he does it because he loves to help people. I think there's also some typical *cop vanity* involved as well. He likes being the go-to-guy for the weird stuff."

Now intrigued the chief asked "what was the cause of the crash?"

"Mechanical failure", North responded. "As always someone tries to profit from tragedy. Bishop had been working a statutory rape investigation with several victims. He built several solid cases. The suspect was out on bond, waiting to go to trial." "After the crash, the defendant claimed he had hired a voodoo practitioner from Charlotte to hex Bishop's family. If found guilty he would do the same to any witnesses who testified or jurors that found him guilty."

"So what happened then?" asked the Chief, Harding seemed enthralled by the story.

"Some in the community were afraid of a curse if they testified. Unfortunately, that's where it backfired. One person who believed the story, was the father of one of the victims. Fearing that his daughter was not going to get justice and the suspect would continue to abuse, he went to the suspect's house in the middle of the night, shot the defendant in the head then took his own life." North stopped to look behind him to make sure investigative activities were still in process behind him before continuing. "Again the stories started, Bishop had hexed the guy back or that some of his friends had."

The Chief of Police being a former street cop and detective was naturally suspicious, asked, "was he involved?"

The detective supervisor shook his head, "I hate to say it, we did look into that possibility. We found no evidence of that. Later, Bishop took a leave of absence from the Department and the district attorney closed out the case. Bishop went out West somewhere."

The chief thinking it sounded like a bad made for television movie asked, "West, why?"

Again North shrugged his shoulders "don't know, never asked and he never said. He was gone for about three months most thought he wasn't coming back. He didn't need to for financial reasons. One day he just showed up in the Chief's office wanted go back to work. He did seem a little different somehow a little more distant, reserved and quiet".

Thinking like an administrator the Chief asked. "Was he fit to come back?"

"Chief Baxter had him evaluated. He was cleared for full duty." North answered.

Having heard the story before, the Fire Chief added, "Bishops assistance has been extremely helpful in several large arsons cases. Like the recent the fire at the high school."

Lieutenant North nodded in agreement and continued. "Bishop has an almost eidetic memory. He has a talent to get people to open up and talk. I've tried to put him back in the detective division. He likes working in the schools and the school board puts pressure on the Department to keep him there. He does have a lot of connections in the school system and to select groups in the community that has come in handy."

A dark Ford SUV had pulled up to the crime scene tape stretched across Montford Avenue and a white male exited the vehicle. Looking around, he apparently found what or who he was looking for. Adjusting a tie worn with a pressed oxford button down shirt he walked up to the yellow plastic tape that was keeping the real world from the nightmare of the crime scene. Raising the tape and walking underneath it Captain Stein Connard, walked towards the crime scene techs who were searching and documenting the area around the body. The techs in disposable booties and blue nitrate protective gloves were using very bright lights to scan the area next to the body looking for even the smallest of pieces of evidence that could provide direction in the investigation.

Intent on their search, the Techs were unaware of the approach of the man in the shirt and tie until Lt. North yelled out. "Captain Connard I can brief you over here."

One of the crime scene techs looked up at that point, startled to see that someone had entered his domain. The redirected pressed shirt and tie paused then walked directly to the Police Chief, Lt. North and the Fire Chief. At the yellow crime scene tape he stopped on the inside of the perimeter and addressed Harding, "Evening Chief."

Chief Harding nodded and replied "Captain Connard."

Ignoring the Fire Chief standing next to the Police Dept. Head, he ordered "North tell me what we have."

Lt. North begun to impart the information so far obtained in the investigation, the shooting, the limited witness information, attempts at a K-9 track and the ongoing neighborhood canvas his team was currently doing.

A Fire Department pickup truck arrived depositing Sgt. Bishop holding a motorcycle helmet on the outside perimeter. Bishop waved at the truck as it did a U-turn and headed south towards downtown Asheville. Yelling to the retreating truck "Thanks Cap, appreciate the ride."

To the Chief of Police's surprise, seeing the return of the School Resource Sergeant, the Captain mumbled "Shit, ████ ████" under his breath then turned back to Lt. North saying, "What is the *Kiddy Cop* idiot doing here?" Not waiting for an answer Captain Connard turned and ducked under the yellow tape walking towards Bishop, directing an aggravated voice at the arriving Sgt. "Bishop you can just get the hell out of here, this has no bearing on you or the school system." Continuing his rant as he walked, "I don't need you contaminating the crime scene or messing up the case file with your Mumbo Jumbo bull shit."

Bishop stopped, standing in the street forcing the Captain to walk to him and away from the observation of others and the stunned Chief of Police. Quickly recovering the Police Chief said, "What the hell?"

The Fire Chief grinned saying, "Those are your kids; I have my own to worry about. Unless you need me to stay I'll go check on Kenneth and see if the family needs anything."

Shaking her head, the Police Chief replied, "No, I'll be alright and catch a lift back to the station. Thanks for the ride out here." The Fire Chief nodded, leaving the two standing at the tape line looking at the Captain and Sergeant across the road.

Looking uncomfortable Lt. North told the Chief. "There's a little bit of bad blood between Stein and Bish"

"I see that," Chief Harding said over her shoulder walking towards her two officers across the street.

Interrupting Captain Connard while he was telling Bishop this investigation was real police work and he had no business at the scene. The chief immediately took control of the situation. "Captain Connard, I don't know what the issue is here but this is not the place or the time."

Bishop was still standing in the street with his arms crossed in front of him listening to the Captain.

Redirected the captain turned to the Chief, "Chief you don't understand, this Officer has a history of involving himself in investigations he has no business in, and mudding things up with his nonsense."

Bishop again made no comment only continuing to stand with his arms crossed.

The new Chief of Police stood in front of Captain Connard and continued in a quiet voice. "One, you will not talk to my people that way. Two, the Sergeant was told to be here, this homicide involves someone connected to the school system. Three, if I understand correctly Sergeant Bishop and his officers are our liaisons with the school system. Correct?"

"Yes mam but you…"

Chief Harding again exorcised her control of the discussion, directing the Captain back to supervise the scene. Obviously madder than he was before, the Captain went back across the street to where Lt. North was pretending to be absorbed in what was written on the yellow legal pad in his hand.

Turning towards Bishop the Chief asked, "You want to tell me what that is all about?" Or should I just take Captain Connard's side when I talk to him, that your full of bullshit mumbo jumbo?"

Bishop shrugged his shoulder and begun with "Mostly I try to stay out of his way. He's not directly over my Unit so it's not been too difficult over the years."

"Years?" "How long has this been going on? Hold on, before you start. Drive me back to the office to my car and explain it on the way. Then get started on what Lt. North has directed you to."

Without waiting for a response the Police Chief walked away from Bishop in the direction of the Sergeant's vehicle. Bishop had to do a short jog to catch up. Unlocking both doors and sliding into the driver seat he began his explanation after his passenger was belted in.

Bishop started, "I guess it started when I came to an incident scene I was close to. Connard was there already. According to some officers on the scene, was telling the reporting officer how to write up the report. The officer seeing me, pulled me to the side and said she was uncomfortable with how Connard was wanting the report written."

"He was telling the officer to falsify a report?"

Bishop shook his head "No, not really it was more of leaving out information in the report. The officer expressed her apprehension to Connard about the way the report narrative was written. Connard indicated to her it was his way or the highway." "In hindsight, I should have talked to Connard, I guess. I was senior to him so I told the Officer to write the report up as she thought was correct and appropriate and I would approve it. That started it. He does not like to be shown as wrong or making a mistake. From that day he has taken every opportunity to show me in a negative light. When someone comes to me at a School event or game with information on an investigation I pass it on to where it needs to go. This seems to bug him that they brought the information to me and not someone else in the department."

The Chief raised an eyebrow. This was contrary to what she had observed and in conversations she had previously with the Captain.

Bishop continued, "Before he made Captain, Connard attended a meeting at the County Court House. The best I can figure out a couple of the jailers from the sheriff's department were going off duty and saw Connard park his police vehicle in a no parking space and go into the court house. They decided to have some fun at his expense. Knowing through the grape vine that there was no love lost between the two of us and knowing about my unintended reputation and association with some of the more unusual parts of the Asheville Community. One went back into the jail and returned with two bags of flower and salt. Using the items to encircle Connard's vehicle in a crude hex circle. Needless to say he had a fit when he came back to the car."

Chief Harding interrupted Bishop. "How can he get upset with you for a prank you had no part in?"

"Well, there is a bit more to it", Bishop continued, "Kind of a perfect storm kind of thing." "Right before this happened a group of young people who felt that the downtown patrol officers were unjustifiably harassing them for various reasons. They posted on social media they had placed a curse on the Asheville Police Department during the Winter Solstice. The night after the car incident Connard was involved in a shooting. Three people were shot, two who needed to be and one that did not. "He was cleared by an independent investigation by the state and the local District Attorney's office but had to deal with the civil aspect and the negative press of the shooting. He tends to blame me for his bad luck and anything that seen to go askew with the Department. "There was also some alleged use of force incidents and employee misconduct issues. Yet like the perfect storm I told you about earlier, Stein Connard hit the right combinations of promotion availability, people retiring and promotional committees to fast track from Sergeant to Captain. Myself I don't think he wants to take personal responsibility." Bishop had navigated the police car back to the station and had pulled in next to the east side of the building putting the car in park. Bishop turned in his seat to look directly at his boss "that's about it".

'Not quite" was the Chiefs response. "Why are you still a Sergeant? I've read your file you've got 28 plus years' law enforcement work with the city alone. Have you not tried to advance beyond being a Sergeant?"

"A few times, but for my own reasons I like being a Sergeant".

"OK, I can see that, what about this magic and psych stuff everyone is found of connecting you with, Especially your Lt. North".

"No Ma'am, I am not nor do I think I am psychic or magical in anyway". Like most cops I have seen some pretty strange things. My great grandmother and grandmother believed strongly in it and they pretty much raised me after my mother passed away and later my father dying from cancer. Grandmother was the go to lady for most of the medical issues back in Tennessee when a regular doctor could not be found. Being willing to listen to people, remember what they said or did, being openminded, good luck and regular hard police work created the magic cop story. Not to mention Lt. North's help. I will admit I have used the rumors to my advantage in working cases some but I have never out and out lied about it.

Chief Harding shook her head. "So you don't believe people have abilities that are hard to explain or a gift as my own aunt used to say?"

"Boss, I have done a lot of research on the subject and have quite an extensive library on the occult topic because of my family's involvement through the years. I have found that almost all things can be explained."

The chief smiled "almost all things?"

Bishop repeated "almost."

"Well Sergeant. I think there are a lot of things we don't understand, and many people are afraid of what they don't understand, including Captain Connard. Thank you for the ride, you have work to do."

With that the Chief exited the patrol vehicle and not looking back at her School Resource Officer Sergeant walked to the side door of the Police Station.

Bishop put the vehicle in reverse, puzzled about his conversation with the Chief. He went on to notify the school system authorities of another Death related to the school system so staff would be ready to assist students who had worked with Samantha. Even though it was late Bishop decided to go and see the mother of his late student and see if she knew if Samantha had been working with her daughter.

R. Scott Lunsford

CHAPTER FIFTEEN
RIVERSIDE DRIVE

Oscar Keith reeled in his fishing line out of the dank water with a dissatisfied grunt. The river rushed too quickly today to be fit for catching. As his father would have told him, "The river runs angry today. Something bad is going to happen." Oscar had learned many lessons from his old man: you plant by the moon; you cut wood for a fire at one moon phase, and wood for fence posts at another. The tips had come in handy. As a second-generation farmhand at the Biltmore Estate, Oscar had helped care for the grounds and surrounding crops. He'd seen for himself the very fence posts his father had cut and set decades earlier. They stood as strong as ever, while other posts erected on the same fence line but set at the wrong phase of the moon had rotted in place. Today, Oscar decided his father was right; no good fishing from an angry river.

He figured he'd go to the estate, even though he was off today, to try fishing in one of the stock ponds. As he packed up his things, he noticed a figure standing near the road at the riverbank's peak. Whoever it was wore a slouchy hooded sweatshirt, the kind with pockets on the front, sporting a ball cap under the hood. *Odd,* Oscar thought, wondering why you would need a hood *and* a hat.

Oscar figured it was just another young traveler passing through Asheville. Kids often stayed at small campsites along the river, usually in hopes of getting handouts from unsuspecting residents. Oscar had met a few recently to whom he'd offered freshly caught fish. He showed the kids how to clean the carcasses, build a fire on the riverbank, and cook them right there. But his wife hadn't been happy that Oscar had neglected to call to let her know where he was. She'd been worried sick, she said, and hoped he wouldn't pull the same thing again, no matter how desperate the vagrant kids seemed.

Today, Oscar had $10 in his pocket and figured the least he could do was offer it to this poor kid before he got into his truck to head to the estate grounds. But as he approached the hooded figure, he found himself face-to-face not with an outstretched hand, but with a cocked gun. A shot rang out before he had time to run.

***

Asheville High School, McDowell Street

The loss of Samantha had rocked the school system as well as the city at large. Bishop had gotten in touch with a colleague at the Buncombe County Sheriff's Office to advise County School Resource Officers of the situation. Before leaving campus, Bishop spent a half hour on the phone with Deputy Jade Cole. She worked with schools outside the City in Buncombe County. Their relationship was strictly professional, but he always felt a nagging sense of guilt when he admitted to himself how much he enjoyed their conversations. He knew they weren't doing anything wrong; his wife was gone, he wasn't dishonoring her memory by enjoying idle chitchat with another woman.

He set out to grab a quick bite at Five Points, the diner where he'd met Star not too long ago. It wasn't far from campus. He thought he might order a chicken greek salad with an iced tea—just enough to hold him over until dinner, but not so much that he'd be ready for a nap. The wait staff mostly recognized him on sight. He chose a booth near the window, and just as his salad was delivered to the formica-topped table, he noticed someone walking slowly across the parking lot toward his patrol car. The person was carrying what looked to be a paint pen, like the type young kids would use to make graffiti tags and designs around town. He squinted against the sun and tried to make out the person's face. He nearly choked on his lunch as the figure came into view. It was Star.

Bishop started to climb out of the booth to go outside, but he decided to hang back instead and watch what she was going to do. She appeared to say something to herself before lifting the marker to scrawl something on his rear window. Then, to his complete surprise, she came into the diner and plopped across from him at the table.

He didn't let on that he'd seen her. "Hello," he greeted. "And to what do I owe the pleasure of your company?"

"I just had a visit with Granny," she replied. "Then I saw your car parked here and decided to check in on you. You OK?"

"You know. Stressed. Tired. Getting over it."

"I see. Been talking to your lady cop friend?"

Bishop set down his fork. "What're you talking about?"

"I can always tell when you've talked to her," Star teased. "Why don't you two just date already? Sure, you're a little older than her, but who cares?"

"That's none of your business," he shot back.

"Everything is my business," she smirked. "All in due time. For now, though, I'm worried about you. Even more so after talking to Granny today. She's quite concerned about this evil that has shown up and your involvement with it. She said she gave you a special root for protection. You do have it with you, don't you?"

"Yes, as a matter of fact I do, but not because of its 'powerful magic.' It's because it's a gift, and I'd be rude not to carry it."

"Be careful," she warned. And just like that, she was gone, saying she was off to some Wicca presentation at a nearby library.

Once he was sure she'd rounded the bend back toward the road, Bishop paid his bill and went out to his car. On his rear window he found small runic script that was totally meaningless to him. He knew he couldn't just leave it on the car, so he pulled out his pocket knife and started to scrape the paint from the glass. But then he stopped. Maybe he should just let it be after all. What was the harm in having a little scribble on the window of patrol car? Heck, it might even be part of a protection spell. The more he thought about it, Star appearing to say something while she applied it to the window and that it was written in celtic rune, convinced him it was in fact some sort of spell she placed on the vehicle. The car wash would remove it soon enough anyway, and he certainly didn't want to offend Star by doing away with her handiwork. A gift was a gift and like he said it would be impolite to not except it.

***

Asheville: Police Station, Downtown

It was after midnight and later than Bishop thought it would be as he left the latest homicide case review. A group of kayakers had found another body floating on the river that morning. Officers had assumed it to be a robbery until Detective Foster spotted a white circle spray painted on an oak tree nearby the shore. The victim appeared to have been fishing when he was shot twice. Investigators knew little more than that for now, though, and this incident seemed to have nothing in common with the previous murders other than the painted circle on the tree.

At the meeting, the head of forensic unit noted that the box Bishop had recovered from Star had been sent to the FBI for examination and processing. Several DNA samples were isolated, but none matched current entries in the nationwide database.

The lab report also indicated that the box was made by heating and hammering steel cable wire forging it into flat sheets. The steel appeared to have been made around 1800s. An FBI agency profiler joined the meeting by a conference call, and suggested that the first killing was indeed connected to the others. According to him, the killer was evolving and experimenting with different methods: a poisoning on Church Street, suffocation at Beaver Lake, and a shooting on the Smith Bridge with the murder weapon possibly having been courtesy of Jeeter himself. Next came the shooting on Montford Avenue, where the killer had attempted to use a homemade silencer made from a soda bottle. Instructions could be found just about anywhere online. Luckily for the police, though, the bottle had malfunctioned somehow and been recovered from the scene. But a fingerprint check showed that bottle had been cleaned with bleach, which eliminated any hope of locating DNA or prints.

There had been a spate of unusual service calls discussed as well: an apparent hit-and-run with a missing pedestrian; an alleged suicide off the Interstate 240 Captain Jeff Bowan Bridge from which no body had been recovered; and a few home break-ins where the only items missing were rounds of ammunition and cash, no firearms or other property taken at all.

There were still far too few answers for Bishop's liking. As he peeled away from the station, he tuned his car radio to a local talk show, "Speaking of Strange." Its host, Joshua P. Warren, was interviewing the author of *NC Ghost Talk,* a recently published essay collection. Given his interest in the occult,

Bishop had known Josh for some time. Josh was an established author apart from his hosting gig and was well respected around town as a knowledgeable Asheville historian. He had turned to Bishop in the past for help coordinating local paranormal investigations, including one of the apparently haunted rotunda at Asheville High. The history around a paranormal investigation according to Josh was just as important as the rest of the research he did. He was the first to argue that it was impossible to get to know a sprit or dead person if you didn't know the first thing about him or her when they were alive.

Tonight, Josh welcomed listeners to call into the show to speak to his guest. Bishop pulled off the road and went to dial but realized he'd missed the station's number before Josh went to a commercial break. He did have Josh's cell number, though, and figured he might be able to respond to a text when he got off air. Josh called Bishop about a half hour later, just as the sergeant was pulling into his driveway.

"Evening, Bish," he said. "What can I do for you?"

"I was wondering if we could meet tomorrow?" Bishop asked, unbuckling his belt before getting out of the car. "I want to tap your knowledge of local history."

Josh laughed. "Well, sure, Bish, but you're just as knowledgeable as I am on that subject, you know. How about seven o'clock at the Raven's Glass?"

"That'll work," Bishop replied. "See you there."

***

Asheville: The Raven's Glass Pub

Bishop was pleased that it was still warm enough to enjoy a brief ride on his motorcycle even as the leaves began to turn in

Asheville. He arrived at the pub around 6:30, rather early, but figured he might as well give himself enough time to collect his thoughts and figure out what, exactly, he was hoping to pull from Josh Warren. The Raven's Glass was a quirky place, established in a repurposed repair garage on a lot of land first built on in 1889. The tavern was reminiscent of a classic English pub, an homage to the homeland of the couple who'd restored the building a decade earlier. Alfred Dymand, the mastermind behind the redesign, had coined his labor of love The Raven's Glass. The shingle hanging out front displayed a Raven sitting on the handle of a magnifying glass. Paying tribute to his years spent as a guard at the Tower of London, and time working as an Inspector at Scotland Yard. Ravens had been housed at the Tower for centuries and required a constant keeper to ensure none escaped. As the old adage warns, *If the Tower of London ravens are lost or fly away, the Crown will fall and Britain with it.*

Dymand had given the pub his own personal touches, like the antique mail boxes that lined the wall of the anteroom. Many of the regulars had been quick to claim their own boxes in which to stash a personal shot glass, mug, or coffee cup, although Dymand had in fact intended for bar-goers to stow their cell phones away so as not to be distracted by technology in a place meant for socializing. Dymand took the use of cell phones and technology in his Pub very serious. On more than one occasion had insisted on users vacate his business or put the phone up.

Dymand caught sight of Bishop as soon as he entered and hollered across the room, "You want your Plymouth Gin and tonic, Sarge?"

Bishop shook his head. "Not tonight. Just coffee, please."

"How about a sandwich to go with that, at least? Beth's in the kitchen and can fix you up somethin' special."

Bishop was about to refuse, focused more on unraveling his investigations than on filling his stomach, but then he reconsidered. Beth could certainly work some magic in the back. "Sure," he chirped. "That'd be great, Al."

Bishop's sandwich arrived at just about the same time as Josh Warren. He knew Beth had been the one to plate it: his roast beef and cheese was the size of his face, accompanied by a heaping pile of red potato salad. No other patron had received such a generous helping.

Dymand turned to his new guest, remarking, "Long time no see, Josh. And what can I get for you?"

Josh motioned toward Bishop's trough. "If there's another cow out back that Bish doesn't plan to eat, I'll take one of those sandwiches and some Irish coffee."

Dymand nodded and turned to grab a fresh pot. As Josh settled into his seat, he draped his jacket behind him and nestled into it. "I've seen the department's been pretty busy lately. Sad thing about those deaths. I know you can't really discuss it, but is anyone close to making an arrest?"

"Unfortunately, no," Bishop replied, taking a generous chunk out of his sandwich. He chewed pensively. "That's kind of what I wanted to pick your brain about."

"Pick away."

"Well, the recent deaths seem to be connected somehow. There's been a circle left behind at each scene—some drawn in chalk, some painted, and one made out of small stones. Granny thinks they might be related to Asheville's history."

"History also shows it's not wise to ignore Granny's intuition," Josh noted, swirling the newly delivered coffee around in his mug.

"True," Bishop conceded. "But I don't see how the locations make much sense, either."

At that, Josh hopped up from the table and made a beeline for Dymand. "Mind if I borrow that map you've got framed behind the bar there?" he asked with a pointed finger. The owner stared back at him, not sure what the question was for. "I won't hurt it," Josh assured him. "I just want to plot out some points to help Bish out."

Dymand handed off the beer he was holding to a customer and turned to untack the map from the wall. "You do realize this is just a framed copy of an old city map from the 1900s, right?"

"Of course. And it's perfect for what we need." He carried the glass casing over to the dartboard area to retrieve a dry erase marker. When he'd made his way back to the table with the 11x14-inch poster in hand, he passed the marker to Bishop, saying, "Here, use this to mark the crime scenes."

After Bishop plotted the points on the glass, Josh waved Dymand over to the booth to join them. "Take a look at this," Josh said, waving his palm over the map. "I can tell you one thing right off the bat, Bish. Your suspect—or suspects—are quite the fan of murder."

Bishop nodded. "Obviously. But what do you mean, exactly?"

"Each of these locations is the same spot where a homicide occurred sometime in Asheville's history. For example—" Josh tapped the mark on Montford Avenue "—two women were killed here in the 1920s. Beaten with a pipe of some sort. No one was convicted of either murder." Josh took a slug of coffee and a forkful of potatoes before continuing. "And Beaver Lake is the location of several suicides and suspicious deaths and one accidental drowning. All in the 1970s. The bridge over the river—several body parts were located there in the '90s. Before the bridge was there, it was a toll ferry operated by the Smith family during the days of the old plank road that ran beside the river. A boat handler was killed halfway across one night by a stranger who refused to pay the toll. On Church Street, a worker came upon a shallow grave while doing renovations. The corpse was determined to be that of a young woman who was murdered over 50 years ago and buried on the grounds without the church's knowledge."

Bishop leaned forward, drawing a pen and paper from his pocket to start taking notes. This was far more information than he'd expected to get, that much was certain. Whether or not Josh's storytelling would hold water remained to be seen. "What else ya got? What about the newest one?"

"The most recent homicide you've marked appears to be the site of Hezekiah Rankins' murder and lynching. He got into a disagreement with a guy who assaulted him with a chunk of coal. They both worked for the railroad at the time of the killing. Rankin went and retrieved a handgun and shot the man, who later died, but not before a group of railroad workers gathered together and forced Rankin to the west side of the French Broad River near the train yard and hung him from an oak. They were arrested but couldn't be tried because there was supposedly too little evidence. The interesting thing about all this, Bish, is that these stories appear on ghost tours all the time. Your killer must know about all that. Maybe the person's been on a ghost tour already."

Bishop perked up at Josh's suggestions. "Hey, what about a tour guide?"

Josh thought for a moment, then furrowed his brow. "Nah, I wouldn't think so," he said. "I know all the current tour guides. I can't think of one I'd suspect. Could be an acquaintance of one of them, maybe, but those circles you mentioned are meaningless to me. Do you have anything else?"

Bishop reached into his leather jacket and pulled out three 4x6 photographs he'd taken of the metal box Star had brought to him. "Ever seen anything like this before?" he asked.

Josh studied each photograph before responding. "Can't say that I have, but the engravings are interesting. How is the box related to the crimes, though?"

Suddenly Dymand piped up next to them, after sitting so quietly they'd nearly forgotten he was there. He picked up the photo of the etching on the top of the box. "Y'all know what this is, don't you?"

"Well, sure," Josh said. "It's a Masonic symbol. But that might not mean anything. You're a Master Mason yourself, Al, so surely you know the symbols might not be related to what's been kept in that box."

Bishop interjected, "Apparently one of the victims had the box and felt that it was causing someone she knew to act strangely. 'Evil,' the girl said. She was trying to find out more about the box, so she took it to a local Wiccan and was killed shortly after."

Dymand shook his head and stood up. "Witchy poppycock. I'm glad I'm outta the business. Gentlemen, your meal's on the house."

Bishop sighed and turned back to Josh. "Well, pal, looks like you've given me more to think about."

"I might know a few folks who can tell me something about that metal box," Josh added. "Let me talk to some people. I'll see what I can find for ya. But," he warned, "I would appreciate some access to a few places later for my research after this is over."

"You got it," Bishop promised.

CHAPTER SIXTEEN
Asheville Buncombe Community College

The last several days for the police department had been busy
for the whole department. Detectives were trying to coordinate
interviews with some students Samantha had counseled. That
meant most of the parents needed to be interviewed, too, or at
least made aware of the course of the investigation so they could
give their consent if their son or daughter was to be spoken with.
Some parents refused because they were afraid their kids would
be dragged into an investigation. Others didn't want their
children's admissions to be allowed in court during trial,
especially given the sensitive nature of some information.
Samantha had worked with mostly troubled youth, after all, so
the detectives' student information pool was relatively limited to
begin with. Some teens' parents couldn't even be contacted to
grant the necessary permission.

Lieutenant North had arranged for the Detectives'
collaboration with specially trained forensic interviewers from
the Department of Social Services. But even with these
precautions in place, Bishop still found himself flooded with
calls from furious parents accusing the school district of doing
too little to protect their kids from the stress associated with the
investigation. Worse, Bishop couldn't disclose much given that
the cases were still open. And so conspiracy theories had been
plastered all over social media: a student was dead, a contract

staff member who worked closely with the high schoolers was also dead, and there were neither leads nor arrests surely the police had to have been covering up something.

Police presence had been beefed up all across the city, and officers working overtime and were getting tired. A break in the case had to come sooner rather than later, Bishop hoped, lest the whole department's reputation go down the drain. He was on his way now to a multi-agency case review and debrief of all involved officers and investigators, those with the City and other agencies assisting, on the current status of the investigations.

Asheville Buncombe Community College had offered the use of a lecture hall to be used for the briefing. This allowed the meeting to be more controlled and secure. When Bishop pulled into the parking lot, he knew he was one of the last arrivals. He made his way through throngs of people—campus police officers assigned to help with security, TV reporters who weren't allowed to be there in the briefing in first place and were being told so, and curious student onlookers who were trying to peer in the windows before being shooed away by campus police.

Bishop entered the building and headed straight for the auditorium. He only needed to nod to the gatekeepers to be allowed in; they all recognized Bishop on sight. As he slipped into the back of the room, the floorboards ceased to buzz with conversation and a hush fell over the hall. At first he thought he was the culprit of the silence until he noticed the Police Chief and Sheriff Duncan approaching the front podium.

They had only made it through a few PowerPoint slides and were just beginning to discuss the metal box when Bishop's phone pinged inside his jacket. It was a message from Josh: *Available for a call?* He was close enough to the door that he could step out unnoticed. He waited until he turned the corner in the corridor to dial Josh's number.

"What's up?" Bishop asked brusquely.

"Hey there," Josh responded. "Nice and professional."

"Sorry," he apologized. "Got a lot going on here is all."

"I'm in Raleigh. Spent the last two days in the state archives, some private collections, and the library at the North Carolina Grand Lodge. This is a good story you got here, Bish."

"So tell me. What'd you find?"

"That box belonged to Zebulun Vance," Josh said.

"The Civil War governor? Are you sure?"

"Sure am. I've got scanned images of sketches of the box that Vance drew himself."

"Was it stolen from a collection of some sort?" Bishop asked, incredulous. "How the hell did it end up in Asheville now?"

"Seems the box was made in the 1800s by the John Roebling Company. You know, the guy who built the Brooklyn Bridge? According to some documents, the box may have actually been made from steel and cable left over from the bridge's construction."

Just like the FBI said, Bishop thought.

"Hang on," Josh rambled. "It gets better. It's not really the box, but what was in it that's the issue—a silver shekel used to pay Judas's bribe for turning Jesus over to the Pharisees."

"Wait, wait, wait," Bishop interrupted. "One of the original 30 pieces of silver?"

Josh relayed the whole tale: the powers the coin gave to those who possessed it, how it had been passed down through the hands of seemingly honorable figures throughout Asheville's history, until finally when the coin was hidden in the box and buried under the floor in the high school's rotunda.

That's it! Bishop thought. And now everything made sense. Granny was right: he had been connected to the box. He'd been within mere feet of the damn thing countless times. Then Brandon James, the rabble-rousing high schooler, must've dug the thing up while doing his community service. And now the box was a part of Asheville all over again.

"So, Josh, this is important," Bishop said. "Do you have more to do there or can you get back up to the city? I'll need your help putting all this together."

"I'll be on my way back in a couple hours. Call you when I get there."

Bishop hung up and immediately called Mountain Lights. As soon as he connected, he asked, "Did one of your counselors, Samantha, ever work with a student named Brandon James?"

"I can't confirm or deny that," the secretary said.

"Yes I understand that, it's Sergeant Bishop, the School Resource Officer. I'm working on Samantha's killing. Can you put me through to someone who's worked with me before, please?"

He heard the woman flipping through papers. "Let me transfer you," she said after a moment.

"Hey, Bish," came another voice. He knew this woman; she was the other secretary. "I can't give you details, but Sam had crossed paths with Brandon before just by virtue of working here. She was in fact assigned to assist the family."

"Which counselor is he paired with now?" Bishop asked.

"Honestly, I couldn't tell you off the top of my head, I can find out" she replied. "I'm sorry."

Bishop returned to the lecture hall. The PowerPoint was just concluding, and he waved to catch Lieutenant North's attention. "Come over here," Bishop mouthed across the room, motioning him over. "Do you know if anyone's had any contact with Brandon James during these investigations?"

"I'm not sure right off, but Detective Foster would know. He's got a good deal of his documentation with him." North relayed the question and the detective was by Bishop's side seconds later.

"I do know that name," Foster said. Looking at his notes he added "It took a while to finally locate him, and do an interview, but friends of the Beaver Lake victim said Brandon was the girl's former boyfriend. She'd broken off the relationship when she became involved with the coven. Then things got creepy because apparently Brandon started following her everywhere. Calling her all the time. Karen's friends said he was like a stalker. He has been interviewed, but no connection has been found with him and the other victims. He provided a good alibi as well."

The tone of the meeting took a sudden change. Lt. North now finally having a tangible suspect according to Bishop, took over the briefing and started giving out assignments to those in attendance. Detectives to back track information on Brandon, even tasking Lt. Lanning, Commander of the Emergency Response Team to bring his people in and be on standby should Brandon be located. The possibility of being armed and already having killed, the department had to take every precaution to protect the community and responding police officers. The team had already responded to several locations in the River Arts District around the old warehouses there. During the investigation, called in tips on suspects and locations came in almost daily and needed to be checked out.

Bishop was also told to work from the school system's end to try to locate Brandon. He immediately followed up with one of his school resource officers who had been on day duty at Asheville High that day.

"Was Brandon at school today?" he asked hurriedly. He cupped the mouthpiece of his cell phone to block out the chatter that suddenly seemed louder than ever.

"No boss, but when I left today, Brandon's sister and a few others were working together on a mural in the first-floor hallway. I know they planned to stay late until the guys were done with football practice. They might still be there."

***

Asheville High School: Lower level, main building

Bishop heard the young ladies before he saw them. He found them using spray paint to add clouds to a 20-foot-long mountains scape. Bishop had been observing its design for the last month. "Hanna," he said sharply, knowing for certain she was Brandon's sister given their stark resemblance. "I'm sorry to interrupt. But I need to talk to you. A minute, please?"

She exchanged a worried glance with her friends before tucking her tools away and rounding the corner with the sergeant. "What's this about, sir?" she asked sheepishly. "Is everything OK?"

"It's Brandon," Bishop said. "Do you know where he is?"

"Why?" Hanna asked. "What did he do?"

"I just need to speak with him. It's important."

"I don't know where he is," she shrugged. "He got suspended and I haven't seen him today. He might be at our aunt's. We're living with her now."

"What's the address? I'd like to go over there to see if I can locate him."

Not twenty minutes later, Bishop's cruiser pulled up at a simple frame house on State Street. Lynn, the kids' aunt, was in the driveway before Bishop could even step out of the car. "What's going on?" she demanded.

"Ma'am," Bishop said calmly, "I'm Sgt. Bishop, Supervisor with the School Resource Officer Program." "I need to see Brandon, please."

"Why are you looking for him?" she asked, clearly exasperated. "What's he done now?"

"I just want to ask him some questions. Do you know where he is?"

"No," Lynn admitted. She seemed defeated. "He's disappeared again. After the fight at school and getting suspended, I haven't seen him all day. He's supposed to stay around here no matter what. I'd asked him to mow this afternoon." She kicked the grass that crept above her ankles.

"But as you can see, he hasn't touched it yet. Can you at least tell me what's going on? Please?"

"Ma'am, I'm sorry to have to say this. But it's starting to look like Brandon is somehow involved with the recent homicides under investigation."

Lynn gasped. "Is he hurt? I promised my sister I'd take care of him and Hanna. She's an angel, but Brandon has been a handful. I wouldn't be able to live with myself if something happened to him."

"Try not to panic," Bishop said gently. "I'll put a call into the station. We'll file a missing person report. That way we'll be able to find him more quickly. Do you have any idea where he might be?"

"I have no idea. Brandon mostly kept to himself. I don't really know much about his friends, but I can call the couple I've met before to see if maybe they've seen him."

A car pulled up behind Bishop's vehicle, and Hanna hopped out from the passenger door, backpack in hand.

"I might know where Brandon is!" she yelled, rushing up to them. After she exited the vehicle pulled away from the driveway driven by one of the older students who had been painting with Hannan. "We passed it on the way home: we had a hiding place and fort there when we were younger, down by the river. Brandon told me a few days ago that he'd been going there to watch the river."

Lynn gripped Bishop's arm. "Please take Hanna with you if you go," she pleaded. "Brandon won't do anything stupid if she's around."

"I'll take her back to the police department," he said. "She can show me where this place is on a map. That way we'll know she'll be safe no matter what's going on with Brandon, if anything." Continuing, Bishop added. "With your permission I would like to have a detective interview her as well." Receiving permission, he and the young lady piled into his cruiser to see where this lead might take them.

***

***

College Street Downtown Asheville

On the way to the police station, Bishop asked Hanna, "Did Brandon have any issues with Samantha at Mountain Lights?"

"No, she was always good to us," Hanna replied. "She was trying to find a special school for Brandon that would help him because he gets so mad sometimes. I didn't think it was a good idea for him to go away, really, but Sam thought it would give him some space, and he trusted her." The strain in her voice betrayed the explanation.

"What about his girlfriend?" Bishop asked. "Was he upset when she died?"

"No," Hanna said, again with that tone. "He had broken up with her anyway. He didn't need her to be happy. And between you and me, she wasn't pretty."

"Still must've been hard with that happening so soon after your mom died," Bishop remarked. "Did she pass away at home or at the hospital?"

"Hospital."

"Hanna," he asked pointedly. His cop's intuition was screaming because of her answers and tone in talking about two of the victims, and even if he ended up being wrong, he knew he had to ask. "Why did you do it?"

Hanna cocked her head to the side and peered at Bishop as though she were lecturing a misbehaving child. "She was hurting and in pain. I just wanted it to stop for her. She would've died whether I did it or not."

Realizing the conversation had suddenly accelerated in a different direction and Hanna was now talking about her mother, not one of the victims as he had been originally thinking, he continued. "And what did you do, Hanna?"

"I brought some of her old pain medicine that was still at the house and put it in her IV after Brandon left her room."

"Did you feel bad?" Bishop pried, wondering about the utter lack of expression on her face and in her voice. She looked completely flat—not like a sociopath, but a shell. Like she would dissipate into dust if he so much as touched her.

"I felt real strange after mom died," Hanna murmured. "I ran in front of a car to kill myself. It was near the high school on my way home afterward, but I wasn't hurt. The cars were smashed, but I got right up and walked away."

"So it must be you who has the coin, then." Bishop's gut feeling had been right a second ago; might as well go two for two. He remembered the person who'd jumped off the bridge but left no body behind.

"I'd been studying its history for a long time after Brandon found it," she nodded. "I was interested about Asheville history in general, but then I kept seeing mentions of the coin and couldn't stop thinking about it. It was pretty lucky Brandon found it in the high school, of all places." Hanna scoffed. "Stupid spot to hide it, if you ask me. Right in the middle of everything. But I took it one day and figured I'd test it."

"Test it?" Bishop repeated.

"On Aunt Lisa's yard man," Hanna responded. "He hung around downtown and always looked at me like he wanted something. ██████' creep. But I talked to him a lot anyway, because he'd give me presents and make me promise not to tell anyone. Like he gave me a scooter one time, no strings attached. But then I figured I had the coin, and I'd read about what it could do, and I thought some weirdo like that would be a good guy to try it out on."

"But why him?" Bishop asked.

"No one would miss him anyway," she said matter-of-factly. "And wouldn't ya know, the coin works. I told him he'd get what he really wanted if he met up with me that night. And I knew he'd show up, cause like I said, he was a creep. So I poisoned his beer, and as he was dying it was like his life was flowing out of him and into me. Like the best orgasm I'd ever had." Bishop glanced at this girl in the passenger seat, wondering what the hell that damn coin did to people. She continued, "Then I went to the bridge and jumped. But it didn't hurt me at all—it felt like I was flying."

"And the circles?" Bishop followed. He spotted a black revolver in her lap but didn't let on that he'd seen it. He wanted to keep her talking.

"What's a circle got in common with a coin, Office Bishop ?" she asked wryly. All artist sign their work."

"Ok but why the others?"

"Samantha was going to break up our family more than it was already. Karen was my friend. She started hanging out with those nature guys and she got weird and started hurting Brandon. That was wrong and like with mom I had to stop Brandon from hurting. I had to. " This was all said like it was obvious and she did not understand why Bishop hadn't already known this.

He nodded and slowed to a stop as they hit a red light. "You think I could see it?"

She reached into her backpack and placed it in his open palm, but not without balancing a pistol also taken from her pack in her other hand. "I bet you've got a vest on," she said coolly, "but I know where to hit you so it won't matter."

"Hey, listen," Bishop said. "That might be tough to explain. You're the only one in the car, you know."

"But it'll be a huge crash," she promised, inching closer and taking back the coin. "And I'll live anyway. You'll have died in a car wreck." The confidant teenager continued, "I thought I had been caught once already, your SWAT Cops caught me painting a big circle mural on a wall in the river arts area one evening. The coin was working then too; the cops in black uniforms and helmets just let me walk out, they had no clue I was the one they were looking for."

Bishop's leg was suddenly hot, and he wondered if this would be the time that decades' worth of policing pressure and not eating right caught up to him. Would he be downed by a heart attack before he could be murdered and left for dead? Then he realized it was the root that Granny had gifted him. He'd been carrying it in his pocket in case he ran into her around town, so he could take it out and declare proudly that he had it on his person at all times. And now the thing was ready to sear a hole through his pants. He took it as a sign also recalling the symbols Star had placed on the rear of his police car at Five Points.

As soon as the next light turned green, Bishop floored the gas pedal and pulled his seatbelt tighter. The Ford rammed straight into the side of a building, and its airbags exploded instantly. The building was in sight of the combined Police Station and Fire Department. Firemen and rescue personal standing near their trucks in the evening air heard and saw the aftermath of the collision and were able to run to the wreck scene before an emergency vehicle could get there. Bishop and Hanna were cut from the vehicle and taken to the hospital. Hanna had struggled against the officers in an attempt to escape, but they managed to restrain her by strapping her to a backboard and watching over her until she arrived in the ER. In response to her objections they told her, she was a minor and without a parent telling them differently they were going to take care of her whether she wanted it or not.

***

City of Asheville Fleet Management Garage; 4 weeks later

Jimmy unbolted the front car seat from the crashed patrol car. Pulling it through the door he saw a flash of something shiny on the floor. Carrying his upholstered prize across the garage, he returned and started looking for what had caught his eye. Not seeing anything of interest, he dug around in the debris

to locate what had flashed in his side vision. Pushing aside what
was left of the deployed air bag he found what had caught his
eye. Picking it up and blowing off the white powder from the
packing material used with the air bag rubbed the object clean.

Jimmy called his boss over to see his discovery. "Boss,
what do you think this is?" Jimmy asked holding it out.

"Looks like an old coin, where you find it?" Was the
answer.

"It was in the floor board of the wrecked cruiser I was
parting out."

The supervisor, Donnie Washington still holding the coin
turned around to look at what was left of the School Resource
Officer marked patrol car. It had been towed into the city shop
for salvaging of anything useful. This included radios, computer
mounts and even the seats were taken out to possibly go into
another vehicle where they may have been in need of replacing.

Jimmy was already thinking "finders keepers" in his mind,
when he asked his supervisor, "What we do with it? Not worth
anything I bet" added Jimmy in conscious effort to say "dibs"
without actually saying it.

Before Washington could answer a voice behind him said,
"Good you found my good luck charm".

Turning around and smiling at the sight of the two men who
had walked in through the open bay door Donnie Washington
responded. "Good luck charm?" Donnie echoed. "I think you
might need a new one, Bishop. By the looks of you, its broken."

"Maybe not," Bishop replied, lifting his casted arm. "I'd
consider myself pretty lucky to get out-a that crash with a
broken wing and nothing else."

Donnie nodded. "Guess so, but you still look like hell, sorry
to say."

Beside the fractured arm the sergeant still had a bruised and
swollen face with a fading black eye, a result of the deployed air
bag. Bishop had hit the block wall of the downtown restaurant
on purpose. If the coin's legacy had been true, and he now

thought it was, he knew his passenger would survive. He was counting on her losing her grip on the coin and hopefully find it in the wrecked patrol car later after they both had been transported to the hospital. The impact had been stronger than he had bargained for. Lieutenant North told him he had moved part of the brick wall back two inches. Luckily Bishop had known the restaurant was closed for remolding and as he approached, no one was on the sidewalk in front of the business. He had a straight shot to the wall.

Bishop reached out with his good arm to retrieve the coin. "I don't think the luck's run out of that quite yet. I may need it back."

Jimmy, who had taken the coin back from his boss hesitated, suddenly thinking he perhaps wanted to keep it for himself. "I'll take it off your hands if you don't want it, Officer. I don't mind."

"That's OK. It's got a lot of sentimental value to me."

Jimmy's boss came up to Bishop. "Looks to me like you'll be out of work awhile," he remarked. "That's probably not a bad thing. You work too much as it is." Washington continued his smiling comments, "I still would go see Granny and get a new one. That hit has bound to have burned out all the luck in it for sure"

"I might be out for a bit, but I can do desk work in the meantime," Bishop replied. "I'd rather not be jobless for long if I can help it."

Shaking his head Bishop's fellow city worker said, 'I read in the paper that your being investigated by the State and the District Attorney's Office".

"It's a use of force issue. I used what could be deadly force to disarm the kid with the gun in my car. Really not supposed to be talking about it." Bishop told his friend.

Stopping at the edge of the bay door Donnie Washington added," I'm just glad the wreck or the kid didn't kill you." Shaking hands Donnie told Bishop. "Man this world is turning into a strange place. Call me if you need anything Bish, I know Granny expects to see you soon."

"I know; she's already sent word". Bishop acknowledged to his friend.

He tipped his hat to the garage crew, tucked the coin into his pocket, and turned to go back onto the street where Josh Warren was waiting for him.

"You got it?" Warren asked, holding out his palm when Bishop nodded. "I just want to see it. I'm not about to touch the thing." He peered at it as the Sergeant held it in front of his face. "Weird, right? How it wound up in Asheville after all that time?" Josh paused. "You sure you're doing the right thing?"

Bishop replaced the coin in his pocket. "Am I doing the right thing?" "This was your idea, you made the arrangements, remember?"

"Yea, but the final decision is yours. You're the current caretaker of the cursed thing at the moment. Well, it's up to you whether or not to listen to me," Josh said. "But that thing's caused a lot of pain over the years. Whether you believe in its powers or not. I think it should be kept somewhere so it can't hurt anyone anymore."

The two had continued walking after the coin had been placed back into Bishop's pocket. Crossing the street and walking towards the parking lot of McCormick Field, the home stadium of Asheville's minor league baseball team the Asheville Tourists. Spying the objective in the parking lot Warren indicated the silver extended cab pickup parked by itself. Often being a host and tour guide in town.

Warren pointed out to Bishop. "You know Lou Gehrig, Jackie Robinson, and even Babe Ruth played ball here. As a matter of fact, on his second visit for an exposition game the Babe got deathly ill and was reported by the media of the day to have died here in Asheville."

"Thanks for the information, now I know what my Lieutenant has been complaining about".

Warren turned puzzled to Bishop and said "what?"

"Never mind, looks like we're expected."

The silver extended cab pickup truck sat running in the middle of the parking area. The lot was used as satellite parking by Mission Hospital. A few of these vehicles were scattered throughout the lot. Standing outside of the truck were two serious looking young men, both Native American. Bishop guessed Cherokee. One had a nylon windbreaker, the other a light hunting style camouflage jacket. As Bishop got closer he could tell the young man on the driver's side was armed, he assumed the other one was as well but because he was standing behind the truck on the passenger side it was impossible to tell. Bishop did not like the situation they were approaching and voiced this to Warren.

"Don't worry, I told you I have everything arranged." The two stopped before reaching the pickup. Warren addressed the closer of the two young men saying, "We're expected here," Josh said.

Bishop noticed that most people in similar situations, standing in the middle of a parking lot would have been leaning against the truck, yet these two did not lean but stood straight a few feet from the truck with a military type bearing about them. Without making a comment, the closest young man stepped to the rear passenger door of the short bedded truck and opened it. Bishop thought they would be told to get into the truck themselves, but was relieved when an older gentleman in a brown leather coat that appeared to Bishop to have been handmade got out. With the assistance of the young man he got out of the back seat of the truck. Bishop had not noticed the elderly passenger due to the very dark tint on the trucks windows. As the young man helped the elder out of the vehicle, Bishop could clearly see the Glock pistol on the right hip of the young man. Bishop carried a compact 9 mm in an ankle holster. He felt out gunned; he did not know these people and was just a little uneasy.

The older gentleman smiled when he saw Warren and extended out his hand. Warren took his hand then hugged the old man slapping him on his leather covered back several times in affection. Separated from the embrace the elder gentleman looked at Warren and said, "You are looking well Joshua" then indicating the baseball stadium behind them he continued, "Are we going to see a few games next season?"

"Of course Grandfather any time you want just let me know." Warren, gesturing to Bishop made introductions. "Grandfather this is Sergeant Bishop with the Asheville Police Department, whom I told you about."

The older gentleman held out his hand to Bishop who stepped up and shook it saying, "It's a pleasure sir."

Firmly Grasping Bishops hand he smiled and said, "call me Tom, or Grandfather, white people apparently get a kick out of calling Old Indians Grandfather." The older man gave Bishop a quick wink.

Turning slightly to look at the armed man holding the truck door Bishop asked, "What do I call your small army?"

Grandfather shrugged and smiled. "Family worries, you know how it is." Josh had apparently already given Grandfather a rundown of the coin's history and all that had happened as of late. "The girl," Grandfather asked. "How is she now?"

"State custody, she has admitted her involvement in all of the deaths. " Bishop confirmed. "She won't be going anywhere anytime soon."

"And the other coin?" Grandfather asked. "It's positively secured?"

"I checked the monument," Josh told him. "It's immovable."

Grandfather grunted. "And what about the other one? Where is it?"

Bishop retrieved the disk from his pocket and plopped it into the open leather pouch the man held out before him. Bishop wasn't entirely convinced that all this was a good idea, but Josh seemed certain that this man knew what he was doing. "You won't even look at it?" Bishop asked curiously.

"I've seen enough evil in my time," the old man said. "I don't care to look it in the face of my own volition. Man's fascination with evil will be his downfall."

Bishop grunted. "So what happens now?"

"The coin will be kept safe," he promised. "You need not worry yourself with how. Now tell me, what happened to the girl's brother?"

"He's carrying around a lot of guilt over his sister, girlfriend and his mom. He tried to kill himself a week ago, but we're getting him the help he needs."

Grandfather shook his head mournfully. "A friend once said, 'The world is a dangerous place to live; not because of the people who are evil, but because of the people who don't do anything about it.' I will pray for him. Just advise me if I can be of any assistance to that young man."

Bishop looked at the old man's hand and the bag with its contents had vanished. Bishop grinned, he was a fan of sleight-of-hand and recognized it when he saw it. "What happens now?" he asked.

"Do you really wish to know?"

"I just want it secured, where and how I guess does not really matter, just that it is." Bishop responded.

"It will be for as long as possible."

"As long as possible? What does that mean?"

Grandfather explained, "There are few absolutes in life." "Death and gravity being two". Putting his hand on Bishops shoulder he looked into his eyes. "But do not worry it will be kept safe and secure and arrangements will be made for that to continue as long as possible."

For some reason this made Bishop feel better, the look in Grandfather's eyes calming some of his fears. And with that, the man nodded sagely toward Bishop and Josh before lumbering back into the truck to return with his men to the Cherokee Reservation from which they came.

Bishop looked at Josh as they drove away, perplexed about the simplicity of it all. "So that's it? I hope you're right about this."

Josh nodded "Don't worry. We're just putting it back into the hands of the original guardians."

"Excuse me?" Bishop asked. "Grandfather's a Mason?"

"Of course he is. Native American Mason's go back to colonial days. It's not a far stretch. I have a book on the subject, if you would like I could send it over."

Bishop shook his head, "No that's OK. I just want that thing put somewhere secure."

Warren continued, "Don't underestimate Grandfather; He graduated North Carolina State University in the 30's." "He worked for the Hercules Powder Company in Tennessee." "Went on to work at Oak Ridge Tennessee on the Manhattan Project building the Atom Bomb." "He's a very smart man and quite capable of many things."

Bishop nodded his head. "OK, what do you think he'll do with it? Hide it somewhere?"

Warren shook his head; "No I am thinking he'll probably drop a mountain on it if I had to guess."

Bishop stopped walking, "You're kidding right?"

"No not really". Was his answer, "He has the skills and the resources to put the coin under a whole lot of very large rock. Same principle as the coin in the monument. The massive blocks of stone protect the coin and if something happens to the monument it will be very obvious. Yea" he continued "I would drop a mountain on it." Warren continued to walk up Charlotte Street with Bishop, going the two blocks north to where he had parked his car. "Now for the current matter at hand," Warren grinned, changing the subject, "you promised me access to some haunted buildings."

The conversation turned to a discussion of spirits and things that did go bump in the night, which suited Bishop.

***

A newscaster stared into the camera. "Emergency Management Director Jason Lambert states that he completed the investigation into the sound of an explosion reported in Cherokee last month. Lambert tells Channel 13 News the explosion is related to an old silver mine off of Bunches Creek Road. Though the sound of the explosion was heard and felt for miles, the mine was isolated and difficult for investigators to find. Few residents even recalled the mine being operational. An older community gentleman told our reporter Nathan Dunne that as a child growing up in the area, he had heard about an old mine where dynamite was allegedly stored in the local hills with children being warned to stay away. Nathan, what more do you have to add to the story?"

The camera cut to a young male reporter on scene. "Well, Janice, Director Lambert tells us that the mine had been abandoned years ago by the family who owned it. The entrance appears to have been sealed to prevent trespassing. Lambert told us it's likely that old dynamite was stored in the mine shaft, which would have become unstable over time. He explained that the nitroglycerin the dynamite was made from had likely begun to seep through the paper casings of the explosive. Even if an animal had managed to find its way into the mine and disturbed the material, the present deterioration may have been enough to initiate an explosion."

"Nathan, was anybody injured in the blast?"

"No injuries reported, Janice. Images from Director Lambert didn't reveal much other than a depression in the side of a hill covered with large rocks. I believe Director Lambert said it best when he told us, 'It's like someone just dropped the mountain on the old mine and it closed up tight.' This is WLOS's Nathan Dunne coming to you from Cherokee, NC."

"Thank you, Nathan. Now on to the weather. Rhonda, what do you see in our forecast for—"

Denise Johnson, director of the North Carolina Juvenile Evaluation Center, minimized the Internet window that was streaming the broadcast. She preferred to have some background noise while reading, although the drone of the meteorologist was unnecessary. She had just finished perusing a thick file on her desk and closed it as its subject was escorted into her office. The female juvenile appeared to be humming a tune but quieted down as she approached.

"Have a seat," Johnson offered.

Hanna struggled against her leg chains to sit in a simple gray chair in front of Johnson's desk. She folded her hands in her lap as best she could. Her wrists were cuffed. This was new territory for Johnson, as the case marked the first serial killer with whom she had ever worked. The young woman's eyes were startlingly green. The green color wasn't unusual, though it made Johnson feel that they did not belong on this young girl but on someone much older. The eyes of the little girl caused Johnson to recall a quote from Ralph Waldo Emerson, "The eyes indicate the antiquity of the soul".

As the two looked at one another, a shiver ran through Johnson's body. She sat up and cleared her throat. "Miss James, the rules have been explained to you?"

"Yes, ma'am."

"Then you understand you will be with us for some time."

"Yes, ma'am, they said I won't be eligible for parole for 25 years."

Life without parole was not allowed when sentencing juveniles in North Carolina, much to Johnson's chagrin. The magnitude of this young lady's crimes warranted more time than that, she thought. "You will be eligible based on your behavior, not the length of time you're here," Johnson explained. "You are not guaranteed parole in 25 years."

"Yes, ma'am."

"And your time here is not without obligations. You'll be expected to continue your education." The young woman slightly smiled at the mention of education then nodded. "Do you have any questions?" Johnson asked.

"I do," Hanna said, suddenly more animated. "While I'm here, I'd like to learn one thing. If it's possible, I mean."

"And what would that be?" Johnson asked.

"I want to learn to play the violin."

Johnson had not read any mention of musical interests in her social, educational and psychological evaluations printed out in the thick file on her desk.

Although the request was unusual, Johnson said, "I'll see what can be done about that while you're in this facility. You'll be transferred elsewhere on your 18th birthday."

"I would appreciate that, ma'am," Hanna said.

Johnson looked up and nodded at the escort that had been standing quietly by the door. She realized that she did not recognize the officer. Someone new or just transferred. She knew she had never seen him around the campus before. The tall man in his mid-30's had one of those faces you would not forget. Like a model in a magazine after the image had been retouched for publishing. Yet he was handsomely unretouched. With light colored hair, neatly trimmed beard and mustache, green eyes and tanned skin under his Detention Uniform. When the Officer caught the Director staring at him he smiled. That was when Director Johnson saw that the smile made him look much older than he appeared to be especially around the eyes.

The detention officer left his position by the door and told the young lady before them, "On your way, miss. We have more to discuss, and then we'll assign you a room."

The officer helped Hanna from her seat and she resumed humming as she shuffled out of the office. Johnson knew she recognized the song from somewhere, and then it hit her: it was a tune she'd heard recently at the annual Bascom Lamar Lunsford Folk Festival held at Mars Hill University every year. The ballad of Frankie Silver, the story of a young woman who was tried and hanged for killing her husband many moons ago. Johnson wondered where the girl would have learned the song. Surely she was too young to have an affinity for Western North Carolina's darker history.

Bonus

The New Novel, Cop and Call
Available in 2017

Chapter One

Mountain Cove near Flag Pond Tennessee 1981

The mottled brown copperhead lunged at the young man, aiming for a sockless ankle poking from a pair of muddied Converse. Its head struck the side of its Plexiglas-paneled terrarium with an unceremonious thunk. The kid ignored the wall of boxed serpents as he trailed behind his mother and father toward a bowed wooden pew in the center of the timeworn church, which had seen many faces over the years.

The white clapboard structure, topped with a tin roof and modest steeple, boasted quite the storied history. It was built after World War II as a Methodist church to serve families in the Tennessee Mountain Cove community, just over the North Carolina-Tennessee state line. After the Methodists abandoned the church in favor of a newer, bigger building, a small Southern Baptist congregation called it home for a short while. Then a family whose house had been lost in a fire moved in to have a temporary place to stay. Years later, Reverend Malakai King of the Gods Mountain Pentecostal Church of Signs finally asked to rent the building. He claimed to be a direct disciple and student of George Went Hensley, who was rumored by some to be the founder of the Churches of Signs and Snake Handlers in the Appalachian Mountains.

The Followers of Sign's belief comes from the literal reading of the King James Bible passage of Mark 16:17-18 :

And these signs shall follow them that believe: In my name shall they cast out devils; they shall speak with new tongues.

They shall take up serpents; and if they drink any deadly thing, it shall not hurt them; they shall lay hands on the sick, and they shall recover. Though a religious practice found in some parts of the south most states had out lawed the activity.

Willie and his parents had attended many services led by Rev. King. Willie liked him, as did many young people in the community; unlike most grownups, Rev. King neither ignored nor patronized the youth of the church. He seemed instead to be genuinely interested in their views on God and the afterlife. Yet he was nevertheless a traditionalist, expecting children to speak only when spoken to as had been preached in the past. "Kids now'days," he often said, "should be seen, not heard, until asked to speak up."

Several of Willie's friends were also regulars at the church, and this Wednesday evening there was a surprise in store. Every service was preceded by a quick chat in which the boys went over the day's gossip: who was in trouble and why, which new pocket knives worked best, upcoming movies and games worth catching, and other essential worldly matters. Before the latest meeting of the 10 and 11-year-old young minds could be adjourned on that day, however, Willie and his fellows spotted something unusual: a pale blue pickup bouncing over the grass to park under the longleaf scrub pines that encircled the grounds. Rev. King came down the steps of the church, shooting a smile and friendly wave in the young men's direction before loping toward the idling truck.

The driver cut the engine and hopped onto the lawn to greet the reverend with a firm handshake. The man's passenger, a seemingly frail young woman who could not have been much than Willie's mother, followed suit. Willie and the other boys were struck by her pallor: she was pale, but her skin was also yellowed as though with jaundice. She and what the boys figured was her husband spoke with Rev. King at length before signaling for a younger boy to get out of the truck as well. Willie and his friends instantly recognized him—Eddie, an old classmate from elementary school—although he was simultaneously taller, thinner, and ruddier than they remembered. He had gotten into a scuffle after school one day several months prior and was seemingly banished from school, as no one had seen hide nor hair of him since. The situation had been peculiar, though, considering that aggression was completely out of Eddie's character. He was normally a quiet boy, even meek, who played ball with everyone and had earned himself a reputation as the school's raven-haired peacekeeper. Everyone liked Eddie... until he changed.

Out of nowhere, during an otherwise unremarkable spring, Eddie became a shell of his former self: outfitted with a real mean streak, a new penchant for cursing and a generally deplorable attitude. That fight was the last straw as far as the school was concerned; the principal sent him packing and never spoke of him again. Whenever a student was brave enough to broach the subject with teachers, they would only say Eddie was sick and they had no idea when or if he would be returning to school. But today, it seemed he was back in town—or at least someone was who looked like him. Rev. King knelt on the lawn, took Eddie by the shoulders, and spoke to him directly while an unassuming audience looked on.

A slight girl donning a crisp, winter white dress soon descended the church steps and rang a red-handled brass bell to indicate the start of the service. The reverend stood to address what the observing young men decided were Eddie's parents, before hurrying back inside. But Eddie didn't move; he merely stayed where he was, barely blinking, motionless as a statue in the brisk fall air. Willie and his mates rushed into the building to seek out their respective families. They were not yet old enough to sit in the back pews with the older kids, required instead to remain with their parents and keep quiet throughout the service.

Willie couldn't help himself and tried to ask his mother what was going on with Eddie. She hushed him as quickly as he'd opened his mouth.

"Tonight's service is special," she whispered. "You must pay attention."

"Ma, but wh—" he started to ask, but his curiosity was stifled by a firm finger to his lips.

"The Devil is coming to church tonight," she said solemnly.

Willie settled back into his seat, not at all satisfied with this answer as the mesmerizing strum of a guitar filled the altar, flanked by chords of a mandolin and electric bass guitar. A pianist keyed the undercurrent to signal that the service was about to begin. Everyone took their seats as Rev. King nearly danced down the aisle in time with the lively gospel tune, which flowed to a stop as he took his place behind the pulpit and opened with a brief prayer. The day's sermon, powerful as ever, warned of evil lurking behind every corner but assured that pure faith would keep the Lord's devotees safe. Willie always had to force himself not to fade during this part of the service, but what was to come was his favorite. Once the reverend's speech concluded, Willie rose from his seat along with the others as music swelled through the eves. Parishioners began to sway to the rhythm and stretched their hands palms-up toward the pulpit.

Rev. King began speaking in tongues. Willie recognized the strange language from having attended a Tent Revival night with his mother. He watched curiously as Deacon Morrow retrieved a handmade box from the collection along the wall and unhooked the securing latch as he carried the writhing creature toward the altar. The deacon left the snake in its case for the moment but removed the outer wooden chamber so the congregation could see. Rev. King capped his tangle of words with a throaty "Amen" that was echoed heartily by the crowd in attendance. He then opened a well-worn Bible jacketed in chestnut leather and proceeded to read from the Gospel of Mark:

"And these signs shall follow them that believe; In my name shall they cast out devils; they shall speak with new tongues; They shall take up serpents; and if they drink any

*deadly thing, it shall not hurt them; they shall lay hands on
the sick, and they shall recover." --Mark 16:17-18*

A willowy woman wearing a sky-blue dress nodded and
said, "Yes, Lord" from the row in front of Willie. She appeared
to be accompanied by a stout gentleman; the color of his button-
down matched her dress, and he bobbed his head in time with
hers as though on a shared marionette string.

Rev. King opened the box on the altar and pulled out a 2-
foot-long timber rattler. He clutched it tightly around its belly,
not behind its head as Willie had seen at the zoo. The serpent
was raised high into the air as the reverend declared
triumphantly, "God is great!"

The squat fellow ahead of Willie slipped out of the pew and
marched to the altar, where he reached up and grasped the snake
several inches behind its skull. He strode down the center aisle
and back again, creature in hand, taking care to keep its head
and tail away from parishioners. Before him, the band came to a
rapid crescendo that compelled the crowd to sing along,
clapping to the beat. Willie's cousin one of the musicians slung
his instrument over his shoulder as the man approached the
pulpit and took the snake from him with an unintelligible holler
that was barely heard over the roar of song. He pounded out a
stuttered cowboy-booted step on the old wood floor in concert
with the tune's rhythm.

Rev. King raised his hands, palms up, and motioned toward
the excited congregation. Willie, meanwhile, watched with
focused interest as his cousin placed the serpent back into its
box and latched it tight. He couldn't remember the last time he
had felt this sort of electricity during a service. That, coupled
with his mother's comment about the Devil's seemingly
imminent arrival, gave him chills.

The Copper Head snake that had originally lashed out at
Willie had discovered a weakness in its habitat. It slithered out
of its container and coiled up under the edge of the carpet, away
from the booming bass of the band, before slinking up to the

pulpit sight unseen once the music stopped. Rev. King motioned to one of his deacons. Mr. Mathews, a lanky man left the church without a word only to return a moment later with Eddie and his parents in tow.

The trio was escorted to the front of the church. As they passed the wall of serpents, every snake began stirring in its cage. Some bared their fangs; others smacked relentlessly against the Plexiglas, apparently undeterred by its imperviousness. The incessant thump!-thump!-thump! reverberated through the small building and punctuated Eddie's steps. Still no one noticed the errant copperhead gliding along the carpet not far from the feet of the perisher's feet. Deacon Matthews presented Eddie to Rev. King, who placed both hands atop the lad's head and began to pray. His parents were ushered quickly into a nearby pew as Willie locked eyes with his schoolmates, whose gazes seemed even wider than his own.

There was an old man sitting in the very first pew to whom parishioners affectionately referred as Daddy Hamilton. He rose from his seat with a grimace, shifted his always-present wooden cane, and hobbled toward the altar where he retrieved a marbled wooden tube not much larger than a coffee canister. He carried the thing past the reverend, past Eddie who appeared to be trembling at the head of the pulpit. The tube's lid erupted with a pop at Daddy Hamilton's weathered hand and a thin line of white cascaded between Rev. King, Eddie, and the rest of the congregation. Willie knew what the glittering crystals were: salt. The wooden cylinder had its place on the pulpit beside an old Bible opened to the Book of Mathew, beside a snarl of freshly cut pine boughs snipped from the trees that loomed over the church. Daddy Hamilton returned it to its rightful place as he doddered toward one end of the salt barrier and unsheathed a most unlikely sight—a thin, long sterling blade—from the hollow of his cane. The knobbed end came unhooked like a carabiner and snapped easily back into place. Willie couldn't believe his eyes. He'd seen the cane dozens of times, even held it for Daddy Hamilton before when he needed to steady himself to take his seat in the front pew. But he had no idea it held a weapon.

In a booming baritone that matched neither Daddy Hamilton's age nor his stature, he declared, "The Bible tells us to be strong in the Lord and his mighty Power. We are to put on the full armor of God so that you can take your stand against the Devil's schemes." Daddy Hamilton drew the long blade along the floor beside the salt demarcation as he went from one side of the church to the other. Once he finally took his seat, the very effort of traversing the length of the building appeared to have drained him.

Willie was fascinated. He turned to his mother and asked, "What did Daddy Hamilton just do?"

"He built a wall of faith to protect us from the Devil," she whispered.

"But where is he?" Willie countered, peering around the room timidly.

Willie's mother nodded in the direction of Eddie and the reverend. "In that boy."

He immediately turned his attention back to Eddie, who was now laid out on the floor, trembling and moaning. He could see beads of perspiration on the preacher's brow as his lips moved in prayer, although he wasn't speaking loudly enough for the congregation to overhear—at least not until he bellowed, "Lord, we beseech you to free this evil from your child! Satan, in the name of God and our Lord Jesus Christ, leave this child! He is a child of God and you are not fit to stand in his shadow. He is protected by God's armor. There is no choice but to leave this holy place; this is sanctified ground. Even the Lord's serpents will not bite the anointed believers of faith and signs, for they even know of the folly of refusing the will of God."

Rev. King sucked in a deep breath before turning to the crowd and imploring, "Pray, everyone, pray for this boy. Pray for his soul to be cleansed. Pray!"

Fearing what might happen should he not do as he was told, Willie bowed his head and recited the only prayer he could remember: The Lord's Prayer. A stolen glance toward the altar found Eddie curled on his side, shaking as though he were atop a tractor motor. Suddenly he stiffened. Rev. King loomed over him, hands raised, continuing to pray as Eddie rolled onto his back and snapped his head sideways just enough to lock eyes with Willie. His mouth rounded into a howl and Rev. King stepped back, looking as though he may collapse.

A parishioner yelled, "Praise God!" and the band kicked up the strains of a joyful version of "I Saw the Light." Willie, meanwhile, felt like he might be sick. His stomach churned and threatened to expel its latest meal. The copperhead that had been slithering along the outskirts of the pews happened to be next to Willie and none too pleased about the sudden explosion of sound rumbling through the air. Without warning the serpent's fangs sank into Willie's ankle as the snake wrapped itself around his stained Converse.

Willie awoke in his own bed with nary a recollection of what had happened at the service. He remembered feeling faint with an inkling that he may lose his lunch all over his shoes. But he couldn't remember anything after that, and no one would mention a word about the rest of the evening. Willie was too nervous to ask. All he knew was that he never saw Eddie again. Sometimes he wondered where his young classmate had ended up, but the town was so tight-lipped about that Wednesday's service that Willie eventually resigned himself to it having been a dream, a subconscious rendering of his deeply instilled fear of the Lord.

***

August 23, 2005
New Orleans, Louisiana

Rebecca could barely see through the torrential rain and screaming wind. She attempted to call for help, but a gust only carried her wail away. Her husband Brian was off with the rest of his firehouse, dealing with damage from the storm. She was worried about him; the storm had proven to be much more threatening than expected. She had taken shelter at a local community center. Her daughters Jennifer and Mary hadn't been able to accompany her, but somehow Rebecca knew they were safe. She didn't feel as though she could say the same for herself, however; a blast of wind had torn the community center's front door clean off, leaving her exposed to the elements in the concrete entrance to the building. She clutched the rusted wrought iron gate and wished for her husband. The nearby river had run over, leaving the water to continue rising in the never-ending rain. It was up to her knees and the sandbags flanking either side of the absent doorway did little to stop its rush.

At that moment Rebecca heard a different sound, one that seemed to float above the din of the storm. It brought with it a searing flash of light and crack of thunder so loud it shook the bowels of the building. The lightning illuminated a wall of water rushing toward Rebecca that had to be no fewer than twenty feet high. It struck her with such force, she crumpled into the mud that framed the old community center.

When she came to, the slick ground had been replaced with the fluffy ivory sheets that lined her bed. The rain had melted into sweat on her brown skin, and the wave that rocked her became Brian's hand on her arm, gently shaking her awake. She tugged the vintage cotton quilt, lovingly stitched by her grandmother, tighter around her shoulders to ward off a sudden chill and reached for a nearby pillow to hug to her chest.

Brian tucked a stray chestnut strand behind her ear, asking, "That dream again, wasn't it?"

Rebecca nodded and tucked her chin into the pillow. "But it was different this time. It actually felt real."

He planted a kiss on her temple and pulled the blanket up to her neck. "I wish I could tell you everything is going to be OK," he admitted. "But I'm not sure how."

The two of them had been together for years before settling down. The men in Rebecca's family had pulled Brian aside when it was clear they were getting serious and invited him to have a drink in their family cabin in the Bayou, where they laid out the expectations that come with marrying a Creole woman. He was nervous that Rebecca's elders would take issue with his background. As one of her cousins quipped, "Brian's so white, he could change oil in a pickup at midnight by the glow of his skin." To his relief, his heritage was a non-issue as far as her family was concerned. Her father once advised him, "It ain't the bottle, boy, it's the whiskey inside that counts. Just don't get to no point where someone feels he's gotta break open the bottle to see just what's inside."

He eventually coaxed Rebecca out of bed with a gentle reminder that Jennifer and Mary needed to get ready for the day. Jennifer was three years old and happy to bounce off to the babysitter, but Mary was only 14 months and needed more coaxing. The girls' caretaker, Sally, arrived shortly after Rebecca began putting herself together for work at the nearby physician's office. Brian would soon be headed back to work at the New Orleans Fire Department. Sally decided to take the girls for a short jaunt in the park so they wouldn't be underfoot while Rebecca and Brian were trying to get out of the house.

As Rebecca contemplated slipping into her scrubs, she was reminded of her family's legacy of helping to heal others. Her great-great-great-grandmother Anne-Suzette Chevalier who had been born to an enslaved woman and her French master in Saint Dominic, now Haiti, and was spirited away during the Haitian

Revolution. Some historians called the successful coup the great slave revolt since Spartacus.

As a refugee child, Anne-Suzette was taken to a Louisiana plantation and eventually learned healing and folk magic from her elders and fellow Haitian refugees.

She had been considered a free woman of color growing up in New Orleans. Yet even as a successful businesswoman by her own merits, some suspected her folk magic past was in fact the source of her good fortune, much like her more famous contemporary, Marie Laveau. Anne-Suzette affinity for the otherworldly had been passed down through generations, strange dreams and all. Rebecca had been unlucky enough to inherit the trait. She was uncertain how far back such visions went, but she did know that her mother and grandmother had each seen their own deaths.

Her mother knew she would die in an accident, which was precisely what happened: a drunk driver jumped a curb and pinned her to the side of a building, where she passed before medical help could arrive. Rebecca was only a young girl of 18 then and had wanted to curse the man who had killed her. The driver later pled guilty in court and apologized tearfully to her and her family. Rebecca could tell that he was truly sorry, and she no longer wished him harm. She became the family matriarch thereafter and made it her duty to look after her family and make a good life for them and herself.

The dreams did not come right away. In fact, it was really just about a year ago that they began plaguing her. She knew her daughters were too young to be made aware of their potential burden and the education of the family ways and knowledge . So rather than warn them of its nearly certain passing, she took to scrawling her dreams and the family history in stacks of journals. She packaged them up as she filled one book after another and mailed them off to a relative out of town for safekeeping. In the meantime, she started transcribing her great-great-great-grandmother's teachings in fresh new notebooks with Brian's help. He even added personal touches to these works in the form of illustrations. He also penned personal notes in the margins to his daughters as lessons for the future. He hoped Rebecca's dreams were just that: imaginary. But Rebecca seemed concerned, and he knew better than to question her intuition.

Rebecca caught a glimpse of herself in the mirror as she tied up her hair and considered how much she resembled her mother. The same toffee skin and dark, brooding brown eyes. She missed her mother fiercely, always had, but somehow felt like her mother was there with her as the girls grew older. She grabbed her purse off the stair rail and headed out to her car for the quick drive to the office. Once she arrived, she went straight into the break room to grab a quick cup of coffee. The newscaster on the TV behind her caught her attention as she rifled through the sugar holder for actual sugar.

"Tropical storm Katrina made landfall in Cuba and the Bahamas last night, causing extensive damage and power outages. Now over the Gulf of Mexico, the warm water is expected to add more power to the storm. Computer projections indicate possible landfall between the Florida panhandle and almost anywhere west along the Gulf Coast."

Rebecca stood frozen in front of the TV, staring at a map of the Gulf of Mexico coastline rife with computer-generated yellow lines fanning out along the coast. One of the lines ended in New Orleans. She fished her phone out of her pocket and called home.

"Sally," she said as soon as the line picked up, "would you be in a position to take the children on a trip?"

"Well, I guess. Where to and when?"

"Asheville. Tomorrow."

Sally's curiosity was nearly palpable. "North Carolina?" she replied. "Why?"

"Just know that it's important."

"But how can I get there, ma'am? I don't even have a car."

"We'll take all of you to the train station," Rebecca suggested. "You can take the Crescent to Spartanburg. One of Brian's brothers will meet you at the station and drive you the rest of the way to Asheville. Can you do that?

"Yes, ma'am," Sally replied. She turned to the girls and said, "Well, kids, looks like we're going to Asheville."

***

Present day, Asheville, NC

Mackey loved to hunt. In fact, he had convinced himself he was a master hunter. After all, he could move silently and render himself almost invisible to his prey. He practiced stalking even when he was not hunting. And his marksmanship reputation was well known, mostly due to self-boasting. He had observed his prey going north and made a broad circle in order to assume a position where he could best intercept it. His target came into view nearly instantly. He drew his gun and fired a shot that traveled across Haywood Street and shattered the storefront glass window just in front of Oliver Griffin. About a perfect shot, if not a hair short.

Ollie froze in place before ducking behind a parked car. He had two men with him, one of whom pulled his own hand gun and began to shoot in no particular direction. None of the rounds came anywhere near Mackey. Instead, he waited for Ollie to emerge from his hiding place. The snitch had gone to the police and managed to get Mackey arrested along with several others who were involved in various illegal activities in Asheville.

One of Ollie's companions finally recognized Mackey and appeared to tell Ollie so. Mackey pointed his weapon in Ollie and company's general direction and fired off the remaining five shots without bothering to aim. Then he ran. Sprinting around the corner, he stopped at an alcove at the rear of a nearby building. He was met by a pile of blankets and coats, the sure sign of a homeless person's resting place. Mackey tore off his jacket and tossed it into the mishmash before kicking one of the loose blankets over it. He stuffed his revolver in a nearby downspout after removing the empty 6 brass shell cases. He would latter drop these in the river to destroy some of the evidence he thought could link him to the shooting. One of the reasons he was a professional, he smiled and thought to himself. Putting on a pair of glasses he rushed away as the scream of police cars came hunting. He couldn't even be bothered to try to cover his tracks better than that.

***

Inside the Haywood Street Book Store.

14-year-old Jennifer was confused. They had been going to story time at the book store when one of the windows near where they stood shattered. Something then knocked her to the floor of the store. Her left leg hurt, and she couldn't move it; it burned like it was on fire. She lifted her head to try to look around and spotted her sister Mary and cousin Justin also splayed out on the linoleum. Their Uncle Joe, with whom the trio lived, bent down checking each of them, gasping a frantic "No, no, no" as he went.

A different figure appeared in front of the kids. "What happened?" Jennifer called out woozily.

The man came over and knelt beside her. "Looks like someone was shooting outside and a couple bullets came into the store."

"Are you a doctor?"

"No, baby girl, but I used to take care of my friends in the desert a long time ago when they would get hurt like you are now."

"Are Mary and Justin OK?"

"Don't worry about them right now," he assured her. "Your dad is taking care of them."

She blinked. "Daddy's dead," she said. "That's my Uncle Joe."

The man then checked on Mary and Justin, to whom he began immediately administering CPR.

The kids' uncle whipped around in a panic. "Where the ▄▄▄ are the EMTs?!" he shouted.

ABOUT THE AUTHOR

Scott Lunsford is a retired Sergeant with the Asheville NC's Police Department. He has over 30 Years public service, 10 Years as a Detective and Supervisor in the Youth services and Sexual assault unit then serving as a Uniformed Supervisor in the Department's School Resource Officers Unit. Lunsford has worked directly with young people in Asheville as well as adults and educators.

He has been recognized in the Congressional Record for his work with the Navy's Youth Sea Cadet Program in Asheville. Awarded the Order of the Long Leaf Pine by the Governor of NC and given a Commission as a Kentucky Colonel by the Governor of Kentucky for his work. Most recently working as a Police Patrol supervisor in Asheville's West District.

Lunsford is a NC State Certified Instructor, teaching juvenile law in the Police Academy, and Juvenile subcultures and issues, through the local Community College.

He has worked as a Field Training Officer in the Patrol Division and Investigative Division of the Police Department, has served as a member of the Asheville Police Department's Hostage Negotiation Team and a Critical Incident Response team member. Sergeant Lunsford has testified in other jurisdictions and States on the information he has obtained and observed in his work.

Lunsford and his wife, retired Officer, Robin Lunsford, have contributed photos and images that have been included and published in *Henry Lee's Crime Scene Handbook*, a Forensics Text Book, by Dr. Henry Lee and Dr. Marilyn Miller.

Lunsford has published articles and photographs in the Brotherhood of Martial Artist Magazine, Martial Artist Instructor Quarterly, The Urban News and the News Record, News Papers. Previous writings include, *Juvenile Subcultures and Issues*, and *There's Plenty of Good Air and Sunshine*. The latter a compiled narrative on his Grandmother and others in the Asheville NC Community during the Great Depression. Originally documented by Lynn Stevens a WPA writer.

Lunsford is currently working on a collection of short stories tied together by North Carolina folk lore, and a nonfiction history book, *Shades of Blue, History, speculation, questions and lies in a mountain Police Department.*

Living near Asheville NC. He resides on a hilltop with his wonderful wife Robin, a slightly insane cat, Bambi the Dachshund and his biggest fan and critic Liberty the Boston Terrier.

R. Scott Lunsford

Cop and Coin A Novel

R. Scott Lunsford

"Now let it work. Mischief, thou art afoot. Take thou what course thou wilt."

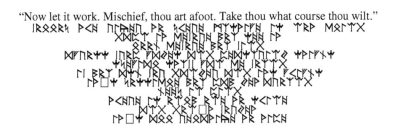

Cop and Coin A Novel

Made in the USA
Charleston, SC
26 January 2017